Christian Girl

TRISH SHAVER

ISBN:1530617642
ISBN-13:9781530617647

DEDICATION

I want to dedicate this book to Lauren Davis. She is very special to me and Christian Girl would not have been the same without you. Love you, sweetie!!

ACKNOWLEDGMENTS

I want to thank my Lord, Jesus Christ for this book. He has given me the ability to write and opened up doors for me.

I want to thank my husband for always supporting me. He encourages me to pursue my dreams and loves me unconditionally.

I want to thank my Mom and Dad for their endless care and love.

I also want to thank my sister, Melissa Spurlin. I throw ideas at her all the time and she listens to me. She reads all my writing and helps edit. She always has my back no matter what. She believes in me.

I want to thank two of my best friends, Leslie Beckner and Donna Crouse. They have both helped me with my new book. They've helped edit and gave me an honest opinion about things when I needed it. They encourage me and give me hope.

CHAPTER ONE
Paige

Paige Jones looked into the mirror one last time to check her appearance. It was the first day of her junior year in high school. She'd picked out a modest blue button up shirt and a pair of jean shorts coming just above the knee. She'd pulled her brown hair up in a high ponytail and applied a small amount of eye shadow and some lip-gloss. She slid her feet into her blue flip-flops that showed off her hot pink toenails, grabbed her backpack and headed downstairs.

"Good morning, honey," Ellen Jones, Paige's mom said while busying herself in the kitchen. "Coffee?"

"Yes, please," Paige smiled and took the coffee cup from her mom. She sipped the delicious, steaming liquid and sat down on the barstool in the kitchen while admiring her mother. Ellen Jones had on her business clothes and her hair was pulled back into a tight bun. She looked like she was ready to take on the corporate world. Her mother was the type of woman who never had a hair out of place and always looked like perfection. Paige, on the other hand, always felt average. Paige didn't dress up much. She didn't have fashion sense, so she just stuck with her usual plain, comfy clothes.

"Breakfast?" Ellen asked, smiling at her daughter and interrupting her thoughts.

"No time. I'm picking up Meghan before school," Paige explained.

"Okay, but make sure you eat lunch, honey. It's not good to go without eating," Ellen reminded. She smiled at her daughter in a loving way and then took a bite of the grapefruit she'd retrieved from the refrigerator.

"Sure thing, Mom," Paige said. "I need to get going or we'll be late."

"Tell Meghan I said hello."

"I will. Dinner tonight?"

"Honey, I'm sorry, but we've got meetings all day and it will be late when I get home. Rain check?"

"Sure, mom. No worries. I'll grab something," Paige said.

"Make sure it's something healthy," Ellen warned. She gave her daughter a fierce look. Paige's father died five years ago of a heart attack and it had devastated both of them. Ellen changed their entire lives after that happened. They started eating healthier and worked out all the time. She was very strict on their diet and exercise.

"I'll do a salad, Mom. No worries," Paige said. Ellen gave her daughter a hug just before Paige walked outside to her car, The Bug. The one thing her mom had splurged on was Paige's car. She'd always wanted a hot pink convertible bug and that's exactly what her mom purchased for her sixteenth birthday. Paige had been ecstatic.

Paige threw her bag in the back seat and started the car. She backed out of her driveway and drove the two miles to Meghan's house. She was waiting on the steps when Paige pulled in. She walked to the car and slid in the passenger seat. Meghan had on a bright yellow top and a pair of tight, white capris. Her black hair was pulled back in two braids going down the sides of her head and she had on silver earrings that dangled. Her makeup was perfect and her sandals matched her shirt. Sometimes, Paige found herself envying the way Meghan always looked. She had to remind herself that envy was a sin and she would try her best to put it from her mind. Meghan was just so put together.

"So, are you ready for the first day of our junior year?" Meghan asked after throwing her bag in the back and buckling her seat belt. She put her sunglasses on and smiled at Paige.

"I guess so," Paige said, backing out of the driveway. She hated her voice sounded scared instead of confident. On more than one occasion, Paige had thought about home schooling just to miss all the drama high school has. Meghan had begged her not to, so here she was, driving both of them to school.

"You know, I think this is our year," Meghan said, sensing her best friend needed some encouragement. Paige laughed out loud at Meghan's comment. "What? I'm serious! This is the year we're going to meet our Prince Charming." Paige almost spit out her last gulp of coffee. Only Meghan would be thinking about a fairy tale on the first day of school.   Paige, on the other hand, was just praying she could find all her classes today and avoid the people who liked to make fun of her.

"Prince Charming? What's he going to do? Sweep us off our feet and live happily ever after?" Paige mocked, trying to lighten her mood a little.

"Perhaps," Meghan said and then both girls giggled until they pulled into the school parking lot. Valley High's parking lot was already busy with students. The seniors all parked in the designated parking area and were talking to each other. The jocks and their girlfriends parked directly in the middle of the parking lot. The other people who drove to school had to scramble around to find a parking place. Paige pulled to the back of the parking lot and cut the car off.

"Why did you park back here?" Meghan asked, giving Paige a pointed look while pushing her sunglasses on top of her head.

"I parked here because I don't want to be in anyone else's way," Paige stated simply. Meghan rolled her eyes, but she didn't argue. Both girls got their stuff out of the back seat and started walking toward the school.

Paige could see a group of girls ahead and Veronica Staples was right in the middle. She inwardly cringed just looking at the gorgeous blonde. She began to maneuver Meghan around the group trying not be noticed, but it didn't work. For several years, Veronica had picked on Paige because she was a Christian. Paige didn't mind anyone knowing she was a Christian. She was proud of the fact, but being called names all the time got old after a while.   Still, Paige walked with her head held high and never let them know they got to her.

They'd almost made it past the group of girls who

looked more like they were ready for a photo shoot for America's Top Model than the first day of school, but then she heard Veronica say something and cringed again.

"Look girls, it's Ms. Goody Two Shoes herself," Veronica said. The other girls laughed at Veronica's comment.

Paige could almost feel the anger coming off Meghan, but she touched her arm and shook her head no. Paige stopped walking and turned toward the group of obnoxious girls and smiled. She told herself she would catch more flies with honey, and tried to remind herself of the bible verse about turning the other cheek.

"Good morning, Veronica. You're looking well," Paige said and tried her best to smile. Veronica had on a short, black skirt, a silk, white tank top and black heels. Her long legs were tan. Her hair and makeup were flawless. Paige felt like an ogre compared to Veronica.

"Yes, I know and you look like you stole that outfit from my grandmother," Veronica insulted her again. The crowd of girls erupted in laughter again. Paige didn't respond to that one. She grabbed Meghan's arm and pulled her along. Thankfully, the navy blue corvette everyone had been waiting on pulled into the parking lot at the moment, squealing tires and took the attention off of her.

Rocky West jumped out of the car and the entire group of girls walked over to him. Jazz, Rocky's friend, stepped out of the passenger side and said hello to the girls. A few girls walked over to Jazz, but Rocky was the center of everyone's attention.

"Wow," Meghan said. Paige only raised her eyebrow, but stayed silent. "What? Rocky West is by far the best looking boy at this school. It doesn't hurt to admire the view once in a while."

"Prince Charming?" Paige asked, mocking her friend.

"Nah, he's far too stuck on himself, but it certainly doesn't hurt to look," Meghan responded and laughed at herself.

"Are you sure about that?" Paige said. Meghan laughed again and they both walked into the school leaving Rocky West and his adoring fans behind.

Rocky

Rocky was glad to be going back to school. It seemed like everything had spun out of control at the end of last year. He needed things to simplify and find some kind of normal again. He needed things he could concentrate on. He had missed football camp because of what had happened, but promised the coach he would spend at least an extra hour a day lifting weights and practicing. He felt sure the coach would start him this year. Valley Run High's football team was in need of a winning season and Rocky knew he could pull it off as the starting quarterback.

He'd picked up Jazz, his best friend, and driven them to school. Jazz went on and on about how much he'd missed at camp and how much Veronica had talked about him all summer and he cringed inside just thinking of facing her. Veronica had tried multiple times to call him and text him, but he'd never responded over the summer. He didn't have anything to say to her and he wondered why that was. He really dreaded seeing her today, but knew that was inevitable.

Veronica had been Rocky's on and off girlfriend for three years now. After everything happened in Rocky's family last May, he'd told Veronica he needed a break, but he knew she would expect things to pick up where they'd left off as soon as the school year started. Unfortunately, he was no longer interested in the type of relationship they'd had. Honestly, Rocky's view on all his relationships had changed quite a bit.

She was waiting on him when he pulled into the school parking lot with her group of superficial friends who only cared about partying and having a good time. Veronica walked up to him and threw her arms around his neck. He stiffened and didn't immediately hug her back. She continued to hug him until he finally relaxed and returned her embrace.

"Rocky, I'm so glad you're here," Veronica whispered to him. "I've missed you." He shook his head, but tried to move slightly away from her. Rocky cared about Veronica, but he just couldn't go back to the way they'd been. Too many things had changed for him since May. He definitely wasn't the person he was last school year. He might still be searching for who he needed to be, but he wasn't the guy from sophomore year. That guy was obnoxious and stuck on himself. Rocky had realized over the summer that's life too short to be like that and he wanted to be a better person.

The rest of the football team had made their way over to his car and they all insisted on bumping fists and talking at once. Rocky welcomed the loud distraction from Veronica. He could tell by the look on her face she wasn't happy about his lack of enthusiasm toward her. He knew eventually he would have to tell her they wouldn't be getting back together, but not today. His first day of school would be focused on classes and practice. That's all he could think of. He didn't want any drama today.

Rocky, Jazz and the rest of Valley High's football team walked off leaving Veronica and her friends hurrying to catch up with them. As soon as Rocky could, he lost Veronica in the crowded halls and found his own locker. It was time to focus on school.

Paige glanced at her class schedule again. She had US History for first period. She grabbed her book, a pen and her three ring binder. She wished she had classes with Meghan, but she didn't. Meghan was taking several AP classes. She sighed as she started walking toward the classroom.

She was completely immersed in her own thoughts when she tripped over something large and fell face first to the floor, hitting her head on the doorframe of her history class. A sharp pain went through her head and she felt like she was going to be sick.

It seemed like everyone around her erupted in laughter, but it didn't really register for a moment they were laughing at her. She stayed hunched over in the floor, with her eyes closed for a moment. Her head throbbed and the nausea continued. When she finally opened her eyes, she met Veronica's mocking expression and her sick feeling grew much worse.

She knew everyone was laughing at her. Some people were even pointing. She wondered what she tripped over but then looked behind her and saw Jazz standing there with a fake look of pity on his face. He must have tripped her. She felt the tears well up in her eyes and quickly started picking up her stuff. She would not let them see her cry. She had to be stronger than that. She asked herself what Jesus would do and knew she should pray for these people.

"Yeah, you should really watch where you're walking," Jazz said. "You could have ruined my new shoes." He started to turn around, but Rocky came around the corner and heard what he'd said.

"What's going on?" Rocky asked, sounding curious.

"Ah, nothing man. This pathetic little girl just tried to ruin my new Nike's by tripping over them."

Veronica started laughing again. Paige refused to let them see her cry. She stood up, but swayed a little. A strong hand steadied her and she looked up to see Rocky standing there with concern written all over his face.

"You okay?" he asked, quietly.

"I...I think so," Paige mumbled, putting a hand up to her head. She could already feel a lump starting to pop out. She knew she would have one heck of a bruise.

"Dude, you're seriously asking her if she's okay?" Jazz questioned. "That's just wrong."

Paige continued to look at Rocky and ignore the rest of them. She saw fury in his eyes, but wasn't expecting what happened next. Rocky let her go and spun around to face Jazz. He grabbed his shirt by the collar and slammed him up against the locker. All the girls gasped when they saw that.

"Apologize to her," Rocky said through clenched

teeth.

"Get off of me, Rocky," Jazz replied, trying to push him away. Rocky wasn't budging. He slammed him against the locker again. "Dude, what's your problem?"

"Do it, Jazz. Apologize," Rocky shouted. Jazz tried to stare Rocky down, but it wasn't working. Rocky was irate so Jazz finally gave in.

"Fine, fine," Jazz said and then gave a withering look to Paige. "Sorry."

Mr. Nelson, the US History teacher, came out of the classroom then to see what was going on. The crowd quickly dispersed and Paige hurried into the room and sat down in the first seat she came to. She kept her head down. She didn't want anyone to see how embarrassed or hurt she was. Her head continued its relentless throbbing. Her eyes filled with tears again, but she held them back. That only proved to make her head hurt worse. She wondered if she would make it through class without throwing up.

"Hey, you okay?" she heard a voice ask her again. She looked up to see Rocky West sitting right beside her. She hadn't even realized he was there or that he'd even come in the classroom at all.

"Yeah, I'm fine," she answered with a shaky voice. "Um. I guess I should say thank you."

"No thanks necessary. Jazz was being a punk," he said and shrugged his shoulders. "So, what's your name?"

"Paige," she replied and gave him a half smile.

"It's nice to meet you, Paige."

Mr. Nelson cleared his throat and US History began. Paige tried to concentrate, but she found it difficult with her headache and the fact that the most popular boy in school had taken up for her and then came to sit right beside her.

When the bell rang for class to be over, she hurriedly picked up her books and headed out the door without even looking at him. She wanted a few minutes alone to gather her thoughts before her next class started.

"Oh my gosh, Paige, are you okay?" Meghan asked, when her friend stopped by her locker in a panic.

"Yes, why?"

"Well, it's been told all across school that Jazz tried to knife you and he and Rocky got in a fight," Meghan said. Paige laughed at that. Would the gossip ever stop?

"No, I just tripped over Jazz's foot and hit my head. Everyone was laughing at me, but Rocky made Jazz apologize. It's nothing really," Paige told her.

"You mean to tell me Rocky West took up for you and made his best friend apologize to you?" Meghan shrieked.

"Would you please keep your voice down?" Paige asked. She didn't want everyone to hear them, but her head was also pounding and Meghan's high-pitched squeal was just more than she could handle at the moment.

"Give me details," Meghan demanded.

"Let's talk after school," Paige suggested. "Really, it's not that big of a deal."

"If you say so," Meghan said. "If you say so." Paige knew that look anywhere. Meghan would not stop hounding her until she got every single detail about the incident before first period. Paige almost wished she could go home now and just hide under her covers for the rest of the day

CHAPTER TWO

The rest of Rocky's day was pretty uneventful. He focused on classes. Thankfully, he didn't have any classes with Jazz or Veronica. He was able to clear his mind and listen to his teachers. He chose not to eat lunch, so by practice he was starving, but he didn't care. He knew he would have to face Jazz in the locker room, but he was ready for him. Jazz didn't have the right to hurt that girl and he didn't intend on letting it happen anymore.

When he'd walked around the corner and saw Paige on the floor with everyone laughing at her, all he could see was Avery. There'd been a police investigation after everything happened. He knew Paige wasn't Avery, but it stirred up feelings in him he couldn't let go of. No one deserved to be treated like that. If someone had taken up for Avery, maybe things would have turned out differently.

He walked in the locker room and heard the loud music. Everyone was talking at once. Jake threw his hand up to Rocky as he walked by to get to his locker where his pads were. Jake and Rocky were friends, but Rocky had always chosen Jazz over Jake because he liked to have a good time. Rocky was starting to question his judgment in his choice of friends. Rocky waved back, but continued walking. Jazz was leaned up against the locker waiting on him. He looked like he was ready for confrontation.

"I'm not looking for a fight," Rocky warned, but there was an edge to his voice that clearly told Jazz he would fight if he had to.

"Sure could have fooled me, man," Jazz answered, sarcastically. "What was that back there? We're friends. Best friends. You don't slam your best friend against a locker just because he played a joke on a girl of no importance."

"Look, I just don't think you should treat someone like that," Rocky said. "And what gives you the right to decide she isn't important?"

"Do you hear yourself right now? Do you remember the stuff you pulled on people last year? Do you remember the way you treated half of this school your entire sophomore year?"

"Yeah, I know and I'm not proud of it. I'm not the same guy. Things change and I don't want you picking on that girl anymore. She doesn't deserve that."

"Alright, but Veronica was the one who put me up to it, anyway. She's always kind of had it out for the girl. I don't even know why," Jazz commented and shrugged his shoulders like it didn't really matter to him. That irritated Rocky again, but he held his temper.

"Yeah, well she needs to get over that," Rocky said, opening his locker and pulling his pads out for practice.

"Look man, are we solid?" Jazz asked. "I'm sorry man. I really am."

"Yeah, we're solid," Rocky answered after a moment's hesitation. They bumped fists. "Look, if you're really sorry, you should tell Paige, not me."

"Okay, but I've got to ask," Jazz said. "Are you into her? I mean I thought you and Veronica would get back together, but if not, I might have a go with Veronica. I mean only if you weren't getting back together and you don't mind."

"No, Paige isn't my type," Rocky said. "Besides, I just met her this morning. As far as Veronica goes, no, I'm not planning on getting back together. You're welcome to her."

"Man, for someone you hadn't even met until this morning, you sure took that personally," Jazz commented with a puzzled look on his face. One of the other teammates slung a dirty towel at Jazz then and he took off after them. They were shouts and running coming from all over the locker room. That saved Rocky from having to say anything else. Even though he hadn't known Paige until that morning, he had known Avery, and all he could think about was what happened and why no one stood up for her. He couldn't let something like that happen again. He wouldn't let what happened to Avery happen to Paige. He would make sure of it. He wondered if she was feeling okay and thought he might try and find out where she lives. It wouldn't hurt to go by and check on her this evening.

By the time Paige dropped Meghan off at her house, she was completely exhausted. She felt like her brain had been fried from all the conversation she'd had to endure from Meghan. She'd analyzed the entire situation and of course painted Rocky as Paige's knight in shining armor. Meghan had them riding off into the sunset before senior year got here. Paige was thankful Rocky had stepped up for her, but she knew it didn't mean anything. He didn't know her and would probably go back to being a self-centered jerk tomorrow. She was sure he wouldn't even sit beside her or talk to her tomorrow and that was completely fine. She didn't need the aggravation.

When she walked in to her house, she was thankful for the quiet. She'd promised her mom she would eat lunch, but she'd been too sick to try and eat anything. She'd took some Ibuprofen and was finally ready to get something in her stomach. Her first thought was to call the local pizza joint and get them to deliver a cheese pizza. She knew she wouldn't be able to hide the evidence from her mom though, so she opted to head back out and pick up at Caesar salad from Gilotti's. They served Italian food and delicious salads. She dialed the number and placed her order. Her mouth was watering just thinking about food. She grabbed her keys and walked back outside to her car.

The drive was short to the restaurant. She pulled in the parking lot and went inside. She told the guy at the cash register she was picking up an order and then sat down to wait on her order at the bar.

"Wow, Ms. Perfect is out buying her something to

eat," she heard a female voice behind her say. Paige didn't have to turn around to know who it was. Veronica Staples was her constant tormentor and Paige had no idea why. She'd never done anything to her. Paige decided to ignore her and stared straight ahead, hoping she would just go away.

"Hey, little girl, I'm talking to you," Veronica snarled and shoved her shoulder a little. Paige could feel the unleashed fury inside, but she counted to ten before responding.

"Well, I'm choosing not to talk to you," Paige said, still looking straight ahead. She was surprised at how calm she actually sounded.

"Rocky takes up for you one time and you think you're all high and mighty now, don't you?"

That did it for her. Paige whirled around and stared Veronica in the eyes. "I don't know what I ever did to you to make you hate me so much and I definitely didn't ask Rocky to take up for me this morning."

"No, but I'm sure you loved that he did. Listen, this is your one and only warning. He's mine. Stay away from him."

Paige wanted to laugh at her. "Will do. I have no interest in your boyfriend."

"Sure you do. Just like every other girl in this school, but he's off limits."

"Noted, now if you don't mind, I have food to pick up," Paige said. She turned around and prayed Veronica would walk away. Thankfully, she did and Paige was able to pay for her food in peace. She felt like she could breathe again as Veronica and the group of girls who followed her around pulled out of Gilloti's parking lot.

"Mean girls, huh?" the guy at the cash register asked

as he took Paige's money.

"Girls who need God in their life," Paige told him. The guy looked at her with a perplexed look on his face for a minute and then handed her change to her. She thanked him, picked up the food and headed back home.

When practice was over, Rocky could feel the tension in his aching muscles. Practice had been brutal. Coach Braddock was hard on him. He knew Rocky liked a challenge, but he felt like this was almost torture.

Jazz told Rocky he was going with some of the other guys to grab something to eat. They asked if he wanted to go too, but Rocky declined. He was thankful he didn't have to take Jazz home and listen to him. There was only one thing he wanted to do that evening.

He waited until the majority of the guys left and then walked around to where Jake was just closing his locker.

"What's up, man?" Jake asked. They bumped fists. "Look, I heard what you did for Paige and I'm glad you did. Girls had a rough life. People need to lay off."

"You know her?" Rocky asked, but he said it more like a statement.

"Her dad worked for my dad up until about five years ago," Jake explained.

"What happened? Did he get fired or something?"

"No. He had a massive heart attack and died. Paige and her mom were devastated."

"Wow, that's awful. So, are you all friends?" Rocky asked. Jake eyed him a little suspiciously, but continued to talk.

"Well, yes and no. When I see her we speak, but we

don't hang out or anything like that," Jake told him.

"Do you know where she lives?" Rocky asked.

"You like her," Jake said. He meant that comment to sound like a question, but it came out as more of a statement.

"I just wanted to check on her and make sure she's okay," he explained.

"Yeah, I know where she lives. When her dad died our family took food over and stayed with them awhile. My dad felt like it was his obligation to extend the condolences from the company. I'll never forget the defeated look in Paige's eyes. She wouldn't talk at all. She sat very still. She only glanced up one time and looked at me. It was like looking at a crippled animal. I won't ever forget that. That's why I'm thankful you put Jazz in his place."

"Yeah, well, he didn't appreciate it very much," Rocky commented.

"Something tells me you don't really care at the moment," Jake replied.

"True. Jazz is my best friend, but I'm glad I could set him straight before things got horribly out of hand."

Jake gave Rocky the address and wished him luck. He strolled out to his car and started the engine. He sat there for a while wondering if he should go and see Paige or not. He didn't want to scare her, but he didn't want her to feel alone either. Finally, he decided he was going. He put the car in drive and headed her way.

Paige walked in her house and sat her salad down on the bar in the kitchen. She got a plate down from the cabinet. She was only going to eat half the salad and save the rest for another meal. She quickly retrieved a fork and knife from the drawer and a bottle of water from the refrigerator. She sat down and was about to say her blessing when she heard a knock at the door. She wondered who would be there. Meghan?? She walked out of the kitchen and through her house into the foyer. She pulled the door open and just stood and stared at the boy looking back at her.

"Um..hi?" Rocky said. Paige still just stared at him. She was completely caught off guard by him standing there. "Yeah, I was just coming by to check on you." Rocky started fidgeting a little and it snapped Paige out of her stare.

"Uh, yeah, I'm okay."

"Well, I guess I'll just go," Rocky said, but he still hesitated, looking at Paige. She looked differently than she did when she was at school. She had her hair pulled back in a messy bun. She had a tank top and a pair of knit shorts. She looked cute, really cute.

"Uh..do you want to come in?" Paige finally asked. She nibbled on the bottom of her lip waiting for his answer.

"Sure thing," he said. She opened the door wider for him to come in. She knew Meghan would have a field day with this. She closed the door and turned around the watch him looking around their house.

"I was just about to eat," Paige said. She didn't know why she'd just told him that. She was feeling very unsure of herself.

"Oh yeah, cool. Go ahead," he said. She started walking toward the kitchen and he followed. She stopped abruptly in the middle of the hall and turned to face. Rocky almost ran into her.

"Do you like salad?" she asked.

"Yeah, salad is great."

"Do you want some? I got a salad from Gilotti's, but I can't eat it all," Paige explained.

'Gilotti's? I love that place," Rocky said.

"Me too," Paige replied with a smile. "So, you want some?"

"I'd love it," he said. She turned around again and finished walking to the kitchen. He watched her grab a plate and sat it down on the bar. He sat down where she'd set the plate. She dished him what was left of the take out box from Gilotti's and handed him some dressing. She pulled a drawer open and got him a knife and fork and finally asked him if water was okay.

"Water's cool," he said. She handed him the bottle and he started to dig in the salad, but stopped with a forkful almost to his mouth when he noticed she was just sitting there.

"I always say the blessing over my food," she said. She noticed the way he looked a little embarrassed that he was about to eat. He quickly set his fork down.

"Oh yeah, sorry," he said. She bowed her head and he followed suit.

"Dear heavenly father, thank you for this day and everything you've done for me. Thank you for this food. Please bless it to our bodies and our bodies to thy service. Thank you for Rocky and what he did for me today. In Jesus name, Amen."

When Paige looked up, Rocky was staring at her with an unreadable expression on his face. She usually got this kind of reaction when someone saw her pray. She tentatively smiled at him and motioned for him to eat.

For a few minutes, they ate in silence, only stopping long enough to say something about how good the food was. When Paige could no longer take it, she turned and faced him.

"Rocky, why are you here? It's not like we've ever hung out before," she said.

"Honestly, I wanted to make sure you were okay after what happened today," he said.

"Look, I'm fine," she started. He gave her a pointed look, but she ignored that. It wasn't the first time someone did something like that to her. "Really, I'm fine." "Look, I just wanted you to know if they pick on you again, I can handle it," Rocky said.

"It's not that big of a deal," Paige protested.

"It is to me," he replied.

"Why? You don't know me at all. What makes you care?" Paige asked.

"Well, I knew a girl a lot like you. She didn't go to our school. She was picked on and ridiculed and I wasn't there for her. Things ended badly and I can't help but wonder if someone had taken up for her things might have been different."

"Are you talking about your cousin, Avery?" Paige asked him.

"How did you know about Avery?" he asked.

"I don't know if you realize this or not, but your life is an open book. Whatever happens with you is news around school," Paige said. Rocky shrugged. "I'm not Avery."

"I know that," he said.

"I mean, I'm not going to do anything to myself."

"Good," Rocky said and Paige watched him relax. "Still, I want you to come to me if this starts again."

"Okay, if there's something I can't handle, I'll let you know," she said. He gave her another pointed look, but she ignored it again. She picked up both plates and put them in the sink with the silverware. She threw the empty Gilotti's container and the water bottles away. She started fidgeting for something to do.

"I guess I need to leave," Rocky said, noticing how uncomfortable she was.

"You're welcome to stay," Paige replied, but she wasn't sure what else to say to him.

"Nah, I've got to get up early and hit the weights in the morning."

"Okay, well thanks for coming by to check on me. That was sweet."

"Yeah, well I'm just that kind of guy," he said and playfully winked at her. She laughed at him. "Oh, you think that's funny, huh?"

"I don't think of you as some sweet guy who just comes to check up on a girl," she responded, teasing him a little.

"Yet here I am," he said, barely containing his mirth. "I'll see you tomorrow at school, Paige Jones." It was the first time he'd said her name and she liked it.

"See you tomorrow in History."

Paige watched as he got in his car and waved just before he pulled out of the driveway. Her heart fluttered a little thinking that he'd come here just to check on her. Maybe he really was a sweet guy.

CHAPTER THREE

Rocky pulled his corvette into Jazz's long driveway the next morning to pick him up for school and honked the horn. His phone buzzed while he was waiting for Jazz, letting him know he had a text message. He picked it up to check and see who'd sent it to him. For one moment, he wondered if it was Paige. Of course that was ridiculous. She didn't even have his number. He wondered why he thought that, but didn't dwell on it as he scrolled through his messages until he saw his new one.

We need to talk. V

He cringed when he read it. He didn't respond to it. He knew he had to talk to her sometime, but he was angry with her right now for instigating the stunt on Paige the day before. If he talked to her now, he probably wouldn't be very nice. He'd end up hurting a girl he'd cared a lot about in the past. He needed time to cool off and to let her down gently.

"What up, dog?" Jazz said as he slammed into the passenger seat, tossing his gym bag to the back.

"What up, man?" Rocky responded, putting his phone in his console and backing out of the driveway.

"We still cool?" Jazz asked him, when Rocky didn't immediately start up a conversation.

"Yeah, we're cool," Rocky responded. "So, what did you do last night?"

Rocky knew that would divert Jazz's attention. He went into a long explanation about where they'd gone to eat, which girls came and how they'd partied it up. Rocky wondered what was wrong with him. He was actually glad he hadn't been there. He wasn't that interested in the whole party scene right now. Last year, all Rocky had wanted to do was party. Now, it didn't seem important. Jazz continued telling about this "epic" night until the school parking lot came into view.

"So, what's up with you and V?' Jazz asked him.

"Nothing, man," Rocky responded. They both looked up to see her walking over to Rocky's car. She looked mad as she swept her long, blond hair over her shoulder and put her hands on her hips.

"It doesn't look like nothing to me," Jazz said, shrugged and left Rocky in the car. Veronica sat down in the passenger seat and glared at him, while she slammed the car door shut.

"You didn't answer me," she accused.

"I was driving," he explained, avoiding eye contact with her.

"Okay, we'll you're not driving now. You asked for some time when Avery died. I gave that to you, but now you're back and you've barely said two words to me. Why are we not back together?"

"I don't know," Rocky said, although he knew that wasn't the truth.

"You care about me," Veronica told him. She knew he did and she was counting on that fact alone to get them back together.

"Yes, I care about you. I guess there's a part of me that always will, but we're over," Rocky said and got out of his car. Veronica was speechless, but she followed him and grabbed his arm to stop him.

"Seriously? After three years, you're dumping me?"

she screamed.

"I'm sorry, V."

"Don't call me that. Don't you dare call me that, Veronica screamed as she sucked in a deep breath to steady her emotions. "No, we're not over. You're just going through some crazy stuff right now. We'll talk about this when you've come to your senses," she said while she stormed off to go walk with her crew of girls. Her entire clique of girls looked like they could beat Rocky at the moment, but he didn't care.

Jazz walked up behind him and said, "That went well."

"Shut up, dude," Rocky said and shoved his arm a little. Jazz started laughing and they walked to school together while everyone else just stared after them.

"At least I finally told her," Rocky mumbled more to himself than anyone. He felt relieved and he hoped she accepted it sooner than later.

Paige pulled into the parking lot just in time to watch Rocky walk into school. She watched him until he was out of sight and then she got out of the car. Meghan was eyeing her suspiciously as they walked toward the school.

"What's up with you today?" Meghan asked.

"What do you mean?" Paige asked, trying to sound innocent.

"Well, let me see. Instead of your hair being pulled back in a tight, ponytail, it's in a messy bun with the tendrils of curls around your face. You have on a lot more makeup than usual. You have on a jean skirt, that's a little above your knee. Shocker!! You're wearing a pink tank top and you can actually see the cross necklace you always wear. Who are you dressing up for, girlie?"

"No one," Paige said, but she knew she wouldn't be able to hide this from Meghan. Okay, maybe she did get up early and pick out something a little more stylish than what she usually wore. Although, she still sported the conservative look more than any other girl at school, including Meghan. Maybe she did spend an extra twenty minutes on her hair and makeup. Maybe she did wonder what Rocky would think of her today about a thousand times already.

Paige knew she was probably crazy for even thinking a guy like him might be interested in her. It was preposterous. I mean he was the infamous Rocky West, Valley High's star quarterback. He could have any girl in the school. Why would he even consider her?

"Excuse me? I'm waiting," Meghan said as they walked through the front doors of the school. Paige continued to walk toward her locker, hoping Meghan would go away. Of course, that wasn't what a nosy best friend does. As Paige started to pull her history book out, Meghan slammed the locker shut. Paige's shocked look didn't faze Meghan in the least.

"Meghan, you could have slammed that on my hand," Paige accused.

"Maybe now you'll tell me what's going on." Paige glanced around and thankfully the hall wasn't crowded yet with hundreds of students going every direction at once.

"Fine, but if you breathe a word of this, I'll never tell you anything else in my entire life," Paige threatened. Meghan squealed and clapped her hands causing several people to turn and look at them. Paige sighed and pulled on her arm a little. "I'm serious, Meghan."

"Okay, scouts honor," Meghan replied, holding up her hand.

"You weren't a scout, Meghan." Meghan laughed at her, but continued to hold her hand up.

"Oh come on, you're stalling."

"Oh my gosh, I can't even believe I'm telling you this," Paige started, giving Meghan a nervous glance. Meghan stared right back at her expectantly. "Okay, okay. Rocky West came by my house last night to check on me. We shared my salad and he told me if I needed anything to let him know." Paige blurted all of it out as fast as she could and then turned back toward her locker. She tried to ignore Meghan's squeal of delight.

"So, does this mean he's into you?"

"No, of course not."

"Well, why did you dress up? You like him, don't you? Oh my gosh, Paige Jones. This is the first boy you've ever had a crush on."

"I don't have a crush. I mean, come on, he could have any girl he wants. What would he want with someone like me?"

"I better not ever hear you say that again. You're the best person I know and you're easy on the eyes, doll." She winked at Paige.

"Seriously, I'm sure it was just a one-time thing."

"Look, I've got to get to class, but text me as soon as history is over. I need details."

"Why?" Paige questioned.

"To tell me how it goes with lover boy," Meghan insisted and giggled again. Paige rolled her eyes at Meghan's enthusiasm.

"Oh my gosh. You're not going to leave this alone, are you?" Paige asked.

"No, I'm not. I'm out. Peace, babe," Meghan said as she turned to stroll down the hallway to her first class. Paige rolled her eyes again as she watched her nosy, but well-meaning friend walk away.

Paige sucked in a deep breath and hurried around the corner in the hallway. She entered the class and scanned for Rocky. He wasn't there yet. She breathed a sigh of relief. She sat down in her normal seat and opened her book. She was scanning her notes when she felt someone sit down right in front of her. She looked up and into the gorgeous blue eyes of Rocky West. Swoon.

"Hey," he said. She felt like her stomach turned flips when he said that. One simple word and she knew she was blushing. Seriously, what was wrong with her?

"Hey," she replied, hating how her voice shook a little.

"How's the head?" he asked.

"Fine, really."

"Good." He turned around then and started up a conversation with the guy sitting across from them. Paige instantly felt silly for being so worried about what he thought. So what if he'd come to her house the day before? So what if he'd even sat in front of her? He asked her how she was and that was it. She felt completely foolish and just tried to concentrate on the lesson as Mr. Nelson started lecturing. He'd just asked her a simple question and then turned around. Nothing more. No epic conversation or flirting. Nothing.

By the time class was over, Paige had worked herself into quite the frenzy. She felt foolish for trying to dress up a little for a boy. The bell rung and everyone started to leave. She watched as Rocky stood, but stopped to talk to someone at the door. She quickly gathered her books and tried to veer around him.

"Hey, Paige," he said and she turned to look at him. "You look good today." She was completely dumbfounded. She just stood and started at him. She didn't say thank you. She wasn't able to say anything. She watched as he bumped fists with a guy she barely knew and walked off. She was pretty sure she would've stood there the rest of the day, but her phone buzzed, snapping her out of it. She looked down to see what Meghan texted her.

So I need details.

Not a chance. Paige responded and giggled a little to herself and hurried to her locker.

Rocky was glad when school was over. He'd tried to dodge Veronica as much as possible. Of course, he couldn't dodge the ten text messages she sent about how much she loved him and how they belonged together.

Once practice was over, he dropped Jazz home and turned down Valley Ave. He went there almost every day. He parked the car and walked up to the iron gate, opening it and walking through.

He trudged the now familiar path. The hurt never seemed to dull. Every time he read the words on the tombstone, it was like taking a knife to his heart.

Avery West
August 5, 1999-May 28 2014

Rocky knelt down beside the tombstone. "Hey, sweetie. It's me again. If you were here, I know you'd tell me to get a life and quit coming here every day," he said, and chuckled. "I still can't believe you're gone. Things won't be the same this year for Labor Day. Who's going to help me beat Dad and Uncle Joe in Rook? Look, I really needed someone to talk to. I told Veronica I needed some time when you passed away. I couldn't deal with all her drama when I'd lost the closest thing I will ever have to a sister and my very best friend. Now, she wants to get back together, but I can't. Then, there's this other girl. Her name is Paige Jones. She's cute in a sweet, conservative way. Not my usual type of girl. People are always picking on her and I lost my temper with Jazz yesterday because of it. I want to be there for her and I don't even know why. If you were here, you'd know what to tell me to do. I miss you, Avery. I wish you were here."

"We all miss her," Rocky heard a voice behind him say. He turned to see his uncle, Joe West walking up behind him.

"Uncle Joe," Rocky said.

"Rocky," Joe answered and patted him on the shoulder.

"I come here to talk to her sometimes. She was always my voice of reason."

"You were like the big brother she never had," Joe responded.

"Some big brother," Rocky muttered.

"None of that. We didn't know the extent of what they did to her until it was too late."

"I'm sorry I wasn't there for her, Uncle Joe."

"I'm sorry, too, son."

"You better get home. Your mother will be wondering what happened to you," Joe said. "Besides, I need some time with my girl."

"Sure thing, Uncle Joe. See ya around." Rocky touched his uncle's shoulder a moment and then walked away. The loneliness crept in again as Rocky left the graveside.

On Wednesday evening, Paige was organizing things in the basement of the church. She and Meghan were starting a new black light drama with the youth group. She was so excited about it. Monica, the youth leader of the church, had been sick, so Paige and Meghan were filling in for her until she got back on her feet.

"Yo, Paige, you down here?" Meghan called.

"Yeah, I'm here."

Meghan pitched in and they started lining the props up and getting the gloves out. The kids hadn't arrived yet, but they would be there soon.

They worked in companionable silence for a few minutes. Finally, Paige started giggling.

"What's so funny?" Meghan asked.

"You are."

"What?"

"You are dying to ask me if Rocky said anything to me today."

"No, I'm not," Meghan argued, but laughed. "Am I that see through?"

"Yes, you are," Paige responded. "Anyhow, it's nothing really. He said hi. Asked me how my head was and that was about it."

"Did he sit in front of you?" Meghan asked.

"Well, yeah, but that doesn't mean anything."

"I know. I was just asking."

"He did tell me I looked good today," Paige said, and couldn't help the grin from almost splitting her face. Meghan squealed and jumped up and down.

Just then, they heard the door upstairs open and shut and the footsteps coming down. It was time to get busy and no more time to talk about Paige's crush.

The teens started coming in and Paige motioned for them to get in a circle for prayer. It was tradition in class. They went around to each one asking if they had a prayer request. Then, someone would lead them in a prayer.

Kaylee, a fifteen-year-old girl who'd been coming to church about six months, spoke up when it was her turn.

"I need everyone's prayers," she said. "Someone asked me to go to a party this weekend and I want to go. I know it's not right and I'll be putting myself in a place I shouldn't be, but I also want to be accepted and liked. I know what's right and what I have to do, but that doesn't mean it's easy."

"You're honest, Kaylee. Temptations come to all of us. The devil knows exactly what he's doing when he tempts us. He knows our weaknesses and what would make us fall the quickest. You're here with us tonight, admitting you feel weak, but also saying out loud you know the right thing to do," Paige said. "We all need to learn from this. Admitting our weakness is okay, because then we realize we are stronger than we think and with God's help, we can overcome whatever temptations we have. Who wants to lead us in prayer?"

"I will," Abby said, almost bouncing as she talked.

Abby was the one in the class who was full of life all the time.

"Thank you, Abby," Meghan said.

"Dear Awesome God, we are here tonight thanking you for just being you. You take care of us and help us fight the temptations that come our way. Forgive us, Lord, for our sins and help us to do better. Help Kaylee and all of us as we struggle with peer pressure. We love you, Awesome God. In Your holy name, Amen."

When the prayer was over, everyone was smiling and Paige winked at Abby. Then, she told everyone to pick up his or her white gloves and get ready to start learning a new song.

There wasn't any time to think about Rocky until late that evening after church was over and she was home. She wasn't anyone's judge, but she didn't think he was saved. She knew they shouldn't be together if he wasn't. The bible spoke plainly about being unequally yoked. She wondered why she was so drawn to him and then thought maybe this was a temptation of her own. She prayed about it until she fell into a deep sleep.

CHAPTER FOUR

The week passed by fast for Rocky between classes and going to practice. He'd barely registered it was Friday, game day, until that morning when his mom laid his jersey out for him to wear to school.

After he'd gotten to school and said hey to all his friends, he stood outside of Mr. Nelson's history class pretending to talk to the people out in the hall. He was really just waiting to see Paige. He'd sat in front of her every day that week. They talked about class, the weather and the usual things to chat about. Rocky didn't understand why he was drawn to this girl, but he was. Thankfully, no one had tried anything else with her since the incident earlier in the week. No name calling or provoking. No tripping or anything harmful. He was starting to relax. He just couldn't figure out why he looked so forward to seeing her every day. She wasn't the usual girl he went for. She was sweet and quiet. She didn't like attention drawn to her and she was very conservative. She was cute in a bookworm sort of way, but her smile would light up a whole room.

He caught sight of her coming around the corner and

grinned to himself. She had her hair pulled up in that messy bun again. It looked unbelievably adorable, but sexy in its own way. She had on a pair of jean shorts and one of her Christian t-shirts she wore all the time. It was blue and had a bible verse on the back, something about doing all things through Christ. She had on a pair of blue flip-flops that matched her shirt. When she walked up to him, he could smell her perfume. It wasn't overbearing, but just right. To Rocky, it smelled like honeysuckle and rain.

"Hey, Rocky," she said and smiled, biting on her bottom lip. Rocky smiled back at her, watching the way she chewed on her lip.

"Oh, hey Paige," he said like he hadn't watched her all the way down the hall. She grinned again and walked on by him into the classroom. He waited a minute before he entered and took his usual seat in front of her.

"So, are you ready for the test?" Paige asked him as the rest of the class hurried in and found their seats. Rocky turned to look at her.

"Well, I guess I'm as ready as I'm going to be," he admitted. "With practice, I haven't had a lot of time to study, but I'm pretty confident I can do it."

Paige laughed and shook her head.

"What's so funny?"

"You are," she said and rolled her eyes.

"Oh, is that right?" he said, but his eyes held a teasing glint.

"Yes, I don't know how you remain so calm and collected about a test you haven't even studied for. If it were me, I would be frantic," Paige admitted. "I've studied and I still don't feel that good about it."

"The power of positive thinking or as I like to call it,

the power of Rocky thinking," he said, looking quite proud of himself. Paige busted out laughing again. Rocky laughed too. "I'm sure you'll do fine."

Just then, Mr. Nelson walked in the room and passed out their test sheets. Everyone quietened down. Rocky gave Paige a lopsided grin and turned around to face the front of the classroom.

He picked up his pencil and began. The test wasn't that hard and he was pretty sure he'd aced it. After class, Paige was stood up putting all her stuff into her bag. She was looking a little stressed and it did something to Rocky. He didn't like that look on her face.

"How'd you do?" Rocky asked her.

"Oh, I don't know. Alright, I guess," she said. Rocky hated the way she sounded so unsure of herself right then.

"I'm sure you did fine," Rocky said, trying to encourage her.

"What about you, hot shot?" Paige asked as Rocky stood and they started walking toward the door.

"Aced it," he said and gave her a quick wink. Paige giggled again and Rocky smiled at her as they walked out of class. "So, are you coming to the pep rally after school?"

"Um..definitely not," Paige said and looked at him like he'd lost his mind. They were walking down the hall now and Rocky noticed several people giving them strange looks, but he didn't care. This girl intrigued him and he didn't want to quit talking to her. Most girls would have jumped at the chance to show up at a pep rally if he'd just ask them to.

"Definitely not? Seriously? It's the hype before the game. We all get jacked up on school spirit and stuff. I can't believe you won't support your team," Rocky said. He really wanted her to come to support him, but he left that minor detail out.

"With all your adoring fans, I'm sure you won't miss little ole me," Paige said in her best Scarlet O'Hara voice. She looked like she was teasing him and he feigned being wounded as he grabbed his heart. Then, he turned and looked at her straight in the eyes.

"I would," Rocky said. He was serious. For some reason, thinking Paige was there cheering him on made him want to do better. "Come on, tell me you'll be there. I won't take no for an answer." She looked like she was thinking about it for a minute.

"Maybe I can talk Meghan into staying after school," Paige said. "You really want me to come?"

"I wouldn't have mentioned if I wasn't serious," he said.

"Okay, I'll try," Paige said. "No promises."

"I'll be looking for you," he said. They had stopped where the hallway forked into different directions. Rocky's next class was Geometry so he needed to go left and he was pretty sure Paige always went straight.

"See you later, Rocky," she said and waved.

"See you at the rally," Rocky responded. He watched her walk about half way down the hall before turning around and running straight into an angry, tall blond. "Oh, sorry." He mumbled before he actually saw whom he ran into.

Rocky looked into Veronica's furious eyes. She must have seen him talking to Paige. He inwardly cringed when he saw glaring at him.

"Seriously, Rocky? You don't want me, but you were eating out of Ms. Virgin Mary's hands," she said loud enough for everyone in the hall to hear.

"I'm not getting into this with you right now, Veronica. I told you we were over. You need to accept it and move on," Rocky said, trying to ignore the rude comment she made about Paige. He knew Veronica was just mad and now was not the time to discuss things.

"So, that's it. You're with the bible thumper. Does your dates consist of feeding the homeless or giving to some whacked out charity?"

Rocky was getting angry and he knew if he didn't walk away he would say something he regretted. He tried to move past her while she continued her rant. She grabbed his arm and he spun around so quickly she took a step backwards. He could feel the fury radiating off of him.

"If I ever hear you talk about her like that again, I'll make you regret it," he said. "Don't forget who I am and what that means to everyone in this school. Paige is a wonderful person, something you know nothing about. If I want to talk to her, it has nothing to do with you and frankly; it's none of your business. If you ever touch me like that again, you'll be sorry." Rocky jerked his arm away from her grasp and looked at her. She looked hurt for a moment, but quickly masked it with an irritated, angry look. She turned around and walked away leaving Rocky standing in the hall. He knew he was harsh with her, but she needed to lay off Paige and get over him.

Rocky turned and headed to class, hoping the rest of his Friday would go better than his conversation with V. He knew it would if Paige showed up at the pep rally. He was going to ask her to go to the game if she showed.

Paige sat in English class not hearing one thing Mrs. Plummer said. All she could think about was the pep rally. Was she going? He'd asked her and every time she thought about it, her face flushed several shades of red. She knew he wasn't the right guy for her, but he just continued to do things that grabbed her attention. He was smart and charming and he made her laugh. Of course, he was impossibly good-looking. She couldn't ignore that. She found herself wondering what it would be like to hold his hand or to kiss him. She blushed even more at that thought. She'd never kissed a guy in her whole life. She assumed he would think that was ridiculous. It's just that the right guy hadn't come along.

Okay, she wanted to go to the pep rally. She sent a quick text to Meghan.

R asked me to go to the pep rally. Will you come?

She knew Meghan would be thrilled. She didn't have to wait long for a response.

OMG. Of course I'll go with you!!!!!!!!! ;) See I told you he liked you. XOXOXO

Paige and Meghan made plans to meet up after school. She pushed through the rest of her classes and went to find her friend.

Meghan was impatiently waiting by her locker. She was grinning at her when she walked up.

"Tell me you're thrilled he asked you," Meghan said, barely containing her excitement.

"He probably ask half the girls at this school to come today. He just wants support. That's all," Paige said. She didn't know if she was trying to convince Meghan this or herself. She didn't want to be hurt, thinking a guy like Rocky would actually be interested in her. Besides, he wasn't right for her.

When they walked in the gym, it was a mad house. Students of Valley High were everywhere, talking at once. The band was playing the Go, fight, and win song. The cheerleaders were already in the middle of the gym, holding up a banner for the football team to run through. It was chaos at its best.

Valley High Cougars were playing the Blue Hill Tigers tonight. Finally, Coach Johnson came to the middle of the gym floor with a microphone. The band quit playing and everyone eventually quietened down.

"Who are we gonna play?" Coach Johnson screamed in the microphone.

"Tigers," everyone in the gym screamed. Paige jumped at the response. This was her first pep rally. She felt kind of silly for not knowing what to expect, but the crowd's enthusiasm was almost contagious. She felt herself smiling and she was scanning the crowd to see if she could spot Rocky.

"Who are we going to beat?" Coach Johnson shouted again.

"Tigers," the crowd answered in unison and the gym erupted with people stomping their feet on the bleachers. The band played a line or two of We Will Rock You. Meghan was beside her, screaming her head off. Paige wanted to laugh at her best friend's enthusiasm.

"Who's going to lead the charge?" he shouted, after the crowd settled down.

"Rocky," the crowd said. The crowd started chanting his name over and over again. The band started playing again. The football team came running through the banner, with Rocky right in front. Paige's heart jumped a little when she saw him. Meghan glanced at her and grinned, nudging her in the side. Paige's face turned a deep shade of red.

He was decked out in his football gear. His face was red from the excitement. The entire gym was chanting his name and two of his team members picked him up and put him on their shoulders. She watched him as he searched the crowd. Was he looking for her? Finally, he saw her. His grin deepened when they made eye contact. Paige felt her face go red again, but she threw her hand up and waved. To her surprise, he waved back.

When everyone stopped chanting, the cheerleaders did a few cheers. Paige was impressed at the way they threw the girls up in the air and caught them. She knew she would never have the nerve to do something like that.

"So, what do you think?" Meghan asked.

"I think it's really loud in here," Paige said, sarcastically. Meghan gave her an incredulous look.

"Seriously, isn't this exciting? You can just feel the energy coming off of everyone."

"If you say so," Paige said, although she knew it was true. Now she knew what Rocky meant about being all jacked up on school spirit.

The cheerleaders faded into the background and Rocky was handed the microphone from the coach. The crowd started chanting his name again, but he held up his hand for them to be quiet.

"Are you ready, Valley?" he shouted. The crowd erupted with shouts and everyone started pounding their feet on the bleachers again. "It's time to go hunting. What are we gonna hunt? A tiger." The crowd went crazy again. Paige couldn't help but smile. "The Blue

Hills think they're going to come in to our turf and take us down. But they just don't know, this is The VALLEY." Everyone started chanting his name again as he handed the microphone back to the coach. The band started to pick up and play and everyone started rushing out to the middle of the gym. They carried Rocky around on their shoulders for the next five minutes.

Paige had never seen anything like this. She watched Rocky as all his crazy fans swarmed around him. What was she thinking? She couldn't like someone like him. This was too much. He enjoyed the spotlight, but she didn't.

"I think I'm ready to go," Paige said.

"What's wrong?" Meghan asked.

"It's nothing. I just want to get out of here," Paige said. "This isn't me."

"Well, I hate to break it to you, but it's going to be a while before this crowd disperses."

"Yeah, I know," Paige said and they both sat down on the bleachers. Finally, the crowd was thinning and Meghan was making their way through the crowd. Paige was content to just follow. She wasn't paying any attention to who was around her.

"You came," Rocky said, walking up behind them. Paige's heart jumped up in her throat.

"I told you I'd try," she said.

"What did you think?" he asked.

"I think you have a lot of people who adore you around here," Paige said.

"Well, if we lose, it won't be like this. They'll be throwing me under the bus tomorrow. It just comes with the territory."

"Well, we're leaving so I guess I'll see you next week," Paige said.

Just then a bunch of Rocky's buddies came crowding around, trying to pull him away. He looked at her helplessly. Paige waved at him and started to leave when she felt a sticky liquid fly all over her. She quickly tried to wipe her face, but it just made it worse. Whatever was on her was all over her hair and face and had run down her clothes. The entire gym erupted in laughter. Paige could feel the tears building up in the back of her eyes.

"Oh my gosh," she heard Meghan say. Paige refused to open her eyes.

"Throw me some towels," she heard Rocky say. The next thing she knew, someone was wiping her face with a soft towel. She could hear Meghan standing really close to her asking if she was okay.

"Hey, you can open your eyes now," Rocky said. She opened her eyes and looked at him. He was smiling at her in front of everyone, but it felt like it was just the two of them for a minute. "You're even cute covered in red paint." She couldn't stop the smile. One of the cheerleaders ran up to her then and started apologizing.

"I'm so, so sorry," Kelly said. "I was carrying the red paint to go put it back in the locker room and someone tripped me." Paige scanned the crowd and saw Veronica looking pretty smug. She could figure out the rest. Veronica, or one of her followers, had pushed Kelly when they saw her walking toward her. "I'll pay you for the clothes."

Paige looked at Kelly and she knew it wasn't her fault at all. She didn't want the girl to feel responsible. She was just as much a victim as Paige was.

"Really, it's okay. Everyone makes mistakes," Paige

told her.

"I didn't see her, Rocky," Kelly said. She looked like she was afraid he would be angry.

"It's alright, Kelly. I know who was responsible for this," Rocky said. He was staring daggers through Veronica right then. Paige watched as she flipped her long, blonde hair over her shoulder and walked away. She could hear the laughter coming from her entire group.

"The nerve of that girl," Meghan said. "I guess it's the girls' locker room for you. You can just jump in the shower with your clothes on."

"I don't have anything else to wear," Paige said, feeling irritated.

"I'm pretty sure I have some extra clothes in my locker," Meghan said.

"Thanks for helping me, Rocky," Paige said. "I'll see you Monday."

"Listen, I know you're probably going to turn me down because I asked you to come here and this is what happens, but I'd love for you to come to the game tonight. I can meet up with you afterwards."

Paige's first instinct was to say no and she looked at Meghan. Her eyes were about to bug out of her head. She was nodding her head yes behind Rocky where he couldn't see her.

"I mean bring Meghan, too," Rocky said to encourage Paige. "The games can be really fun and I'll lay the law down before you get there. They'll know not to mess with you tonight. What do you say?"

"Okay, but if this game is boring, I'm leaving early," Paige said, trying to tease him. He pretended to be wounded by her words.

"I'll do my very best to keep it interesting," he said. "Give me your phone."

"Why?"

"So, I can get a hold of you or you can get a hold of me after the game," he said. Paige reluctantly handed him her phone. He punched his number into her contacts and did the same in his phone. "Okay, I'll let you get cleaned up and I'll see you tonight."

"See you later," Paige answered back. She watched as he walked away and then Meghan led her back to the locker room.

"Oh my gosh. He just asked you out on a date," Meghan said.

"No, it's not a date," Paige argued.

"What would you call it? He asked you to come to the game and then he's meeting up with you after the game."

"Not a date," Paige said.

"So, are you telling your mom you'll be out late?" Meghan asked.

"She's on a business trip. I'll just text her," Paige explained. "She'll be surprised I'm not in bed by 9."

"Wow, you know how to live on the wild side," Meghan sarcastically said.

Paige continued her shower without saying anything else. She thought about what Meghan said. No, it wasn't a date. He just wanted to be friends. He told Meghan to come too. It wasn't a date. There was no reason to think it was.

CHAPTER FIVE

Paige went home after getting the red paint washed off and borrowing Meghan's clothes. She didn't let herself cry until she was alone. She just didn't understand why those girls were mean to her. She was God's child and she knew any kind of harassment she dealt with was nothing compared to everything Jesus went through for her. She should be thankful to suffer in his name's sake. It didn't mean it was easy to take, though and she was human.

She cried until her eyes were puffy and then she knew she had to quit. Rocky had taken up for her again. He wasn't going to let anything else like this happen. She tried to have confidence that people would listen to him. Most importantly, God was there for her. It was just paint. It washed off. No harm was done. She told herself to let it go. She told herself it didn't matter the entire school had seen her humiliation and laughed at her expense.

The moment she thought of Rocky, her insides turned to jelly. He'd told her she looked cute, even in red paint. She couldn't ignore the fact that her stomach felt like it flipped inside out when he said that to her. She was sure she blushed. It just hadn't been noticeable underneath the red paint.

She tried to tell herself he was just being nice to her. It didn't mean anything to him. He was just trying to make her feel better about having red paint dumped all over her. She knew he just asked her to the game to be nice, too. She told herself not to be excited about the invite. It was just a football game and he might not even remember telling her they would meet after the game. She looked through her closet wondering what an appropriate outfit for a football game would be. She really had no idea. She thumbed through several of her t-shirts, but nothing really stuck out to her. She finally decided to give up and call reinforcements.

Paige called Meghan and told her to come over and help with her wardrobe problems. Meghan brought over a pair of her tan colored shorts and a navy blue tank top for Paige to put on. Paige gave her an incredulous look when she saw the shorts.

"Those shorts are too short for me to wear," Paige argued.

"Fine, wear your own shorts. I'll wear these," Meghan said and shrugged her shoulders. Paige opted for a pair of jean shorts and then fixed her hair up and put on some makeup. She didn't put much on because it was going to be hot.

"Seriously, that's all the makeup you're putting on?" Meghan asked.

"I told you this wasn't a date and besides, it will be hot and sticky outside. I don't want to worry about my mascara or eyeliner running all over my face," Paige answered.

"Okay, I see your point," Meghan conceded. "Do you

mind if I fix my hair in your bathroom?"

"Of course I don't mind," Paige answered her best friend. Meghan walked into the bathroom leaving Paige alone with her nerves. She decided the best way to calm herself down was to read her bible. She hadn't read any today and she assumed she would be home late, so she picked it up and started skimming through until a scripture caught her eye.

2 Corinthians 6: 14:

Be ye not unequally yoked together with unbelievers: for what fellowship hath righteousness with unrighteousness? And what communion have light with darkness?

There it was in black and white. Paige couldn't be with Rocky if he wasn't a Christian. She felt a stab of hurt deep in her chest, but she knew she had to do what the bible said. They could be friends, but nothing more. She had to accept that and not dwell on him all the time and frankly he was consuming a lot of her thoughts right now. God would send her the right guy when it was time. She just had to pray about it and give it over completely to him.

Meghan walked out of the bathroom right then looking like a super model as always. Paige shook her head.

"What? Too much?" Meghan asked. Her hair was perfectly curled and every piece was in place. Her makeup was perfection.

"No, it's just right," Paige complimented.

"Are you okay?" Meghan asked, seeing the forlorn look on her friend's face.

"Yeah, I'm great. Let's get to this game," Paige said, plastering a bright smile on her face.

"Woo Hoo. Go cougars," Meghan shouted and Paige had to laugh at her friend's crazy antics.

Rocky was standing in the locker room listening to the guys around him. He, with the help of Jake, had put out the word. No one was to mess with Paige or Meghan tonight at the game or they would deal with him directly. He knew Veronica was to blame for the paint incident, he just couldn't prove it. It made him sick to think she would do that to someone. What was wrong with her and what had he ever seen in her as a girlfriend?

When he'd seen the paint splash all over Paige, all he could see was flashes of Avery. He could still see the photographs and the blood. He couldn't shake it. He'd barely spoken a word to the team. He was just staring off into space.

"Yo, man. You ready for the game?" Jazz asked, as he walked up to him and nudged him slightly.

"Did you know they were going to do that to Paige?"

"What? Spill the paint? Kelly tripped. You heard her. She was falling all over your little Christian friend, telling her she was sorry. She had the paint because they used it for the banner earlier that day. No harm. No foul."

"First of all, her name is Paige and secondly, it wasn't an accident."

"Look, man. I don't care what her name is or if Kelly dumped that paint on her. All I care about right now is that you make sure your head's in the game. Is it?" Jazz stared at him and Rocky felt the sudden urge to punch him in the face. He didn't act on it, though. He simply stared back for a minute.

"Yeah, man. My head is exactly where it needs to be. We're going kick some Tigers to the curb tonight." Jazz held up his fist to bump Rocky's.

"You're coming to the river after the game, right?"

"I don't know. Maybe."

"Rocky, I don't know what's gotten into you lately, but this is your team. They support you. If you start acting all stand offish like you're too good to hang with us, well your team might quit giving you the support you need." Rocky knew that this was more than a subtle warning from a friend. "You can kiss your precious scholarship goodbye then."

"I've always got my team's back," Rocky said.

"You better," Jazz threatened. "Just saying."

The team started to head out to the field and Jazz followed them. Rocky held back and Jake walked up beside him.

"Don't listen to him. Jazz has always been jealous of you. This team knows how good you are and they know you're here for them. You're not going to lose your support," Jake said.

"Thanks, man. I needed that."

"Is Paige okay?"

"She seemed okay, but I'm not really sure. She's supposed to be here tonight," Rocky said. He couldn't help a small smile that formed when he thought of her sitting in the bleachers cheering for him.

"Okay, I'm going to ask you again. Do you have a thing for this girl?"

"Maybe. I don't know. I do seem to want to come to her rescue all the time and she's interesting. I like talking to her."

"Well, she's a good girl. You could do a lot worse,"

Jake told him. "Oh wait a minute, you already have. V."
Jake laughed at his own joke and Rocky cracked a smile.

"You're going to pay for that one, man," Rocky
threatened.

"Bring it on," Jake teased.

"Don't tempt me," Rocky replied and then laughed
again.

They both walked out of the locker room to the
sideline. Rocky scanned the crowd until he spotted her.
She was talking to Meghan and she was smiling. That
was a good thing. He didn't want her upset.

"Yeah, you've totally got a thing for her," Jake said
and ribbed him. Rocky rolled his eyes. He didn't even
feel the ribbing because of the pads. Jake was right,
though. He had a thing for her.

He shook his head and started his breathing exercises.
In. Out. In. Out. It was his way of blocking out
everything around him. The coach was telling them the
plays to start out with and Rocky could feel his
excitement rising. This was his game. His team. His
field. He was getting in the zone. The Tigers were going
down. He pushed away thoughts of Avery as he
continued his breathing exercises. Thoughts of Veronica
being mean to Paige left. Thoughts of Paige's smile, her
trusting look and the hurt he saw in her eyes when
someone did something to her finally dispersed, leaving
him with only thoughts of football and the game at hand.
His entire team looked to him for leadership and
guidance. When they took the field, Valley High's
crowd went wild. He didn't look up to see who was
cheering. He had to focus on the game. The band was
playing a song and he could hear the cheerleaders in the
background, but all that mattered was the ball and the

game. Go. Fight. Win. Beat the Tigers.

Paige couldn't believe how exciting a football game was. Rocky was unbelievable, just like she knew he would be. They had beaten the Tigers 42 to 7. The crowd went crazy when the buzzer signaled the end of the game. The band started playing some upbeat song Paige couldn't quite place. The crowd started rushing out on the field. It looked like a mob surrounding the team.

"Have you ever seen anything so crazy?" Paige asked Meghan.

"Have you ever seen anything more fun?" Meghan asked her right back. Paige smiled. It was fun. This was fun. Why had she never come to one of the games before? Meghan had asked her on more than one occasion, but she knew why. She tried to avoid people every way she could.

"Well, if we leave now, we can beat the crowd since everyone seems to be out on the field," Paige said and motioned toward the emptying bleachers.

"What? I thought you and Rocky were meeting up after the game." Meghan looked at Paige and saw the disappointed look on her face. "Did he text you and tell you he wasn't meeting you?"

"No."

"Then, why are you bailing on him?" Meghan asked.

"Look, while you were fixing your hair, I read a few scriptures in the bible. It said you can't be unequally yoked. He doesn't go to church. He's not a Christian. That means I can't be with him. What's the point in even thinking about something like that when it can't happen? I'm not sure he even likes me, you know like that," Paige said. She had a torn expression on her face. "The truth is. I do like him. A Lot. I think about him all the time and I can't get stuck on a guy when he's all wrong for me."

"Aww..sweetie. I'm so sorry. I've been encouraging you with this as well. I should have thought about it."

"He's a great guy. He really is," Paige said. "What am I saying? He probably just feels bad for the loser girl who gets picked on all the time."

"Yeah, a great guy who's stood up for you on more than occasion. You're not some loser girl. I know he doesn't think that. He doesn't deserve to be stood up. You can at least talk to him and maybe explain things."

"Yeah, I'll wait around and see if he texts," Paige said.

Paige and Meghan walked out to the car. Meghan sat on the hood and Paige propped herself up, fiddling with her hands. They watched the crowd as they came out and went to their cars. Everyone was lively and excited. People were smiling and giving each other high fives. Paige caught herself smiling several times just watching other people. It had been about thirty minutes when her phone went off. It was a text message. Paige's heart skipped a beat as she pulled her phone out and read her message.

Where r u?

At my car.

Be right there.

"He's coming," Paige said. Meghan slid off the hood of the car.

"I think I'll go find someone else to talk to," Meghan said. "Text me if you need me."

"Sure." Paige waited around another ten minutes when she saw him walking toward her. He changed out of his uniform. His hair was wet. She figured he'd taken a quick shower. He seemed so full of life and energy. He was smiling. Why did he have to be so handsome?

"Paige," he said and smiled at her.

"Hey. You were great out there," she responded.

"Nah," Rocky said, but he smiled at the compliment. "I'm really glad you came. Maybe you're my good luck charm. Listen, the team and their girls are heading down to the river. It's tradition. We do it after every game. I wasn't even sure I wanted to go tonight, but after our mega victory, I'm going. Do you want to come? We don't even have to stay long if you don't want to."

"Um…well," Paige started to reply, but he interrupted.

"I probably need to make myself clear. I'm not asking you as my friend. I'm asking you as my date. Paige Jones, you are the most amazing person I've ever known. Will you be my date tonight?"

Paige felt tears sting the back of her eyes. No one had ever said anything that sweet to her. How could she turn him down? How could she go? Why was it the only guy who'd ever paid attention to her was someone she couldn't be with?

"Rocky, I'm so sorry. I can't," Paige said. Rocky looked at her a moment before saying anything.

"Did you have something else already planned?"

"No."

"Then, of course you can. No one will mess with you as long as you're with me."

"I can't go out with you. I can't go to the river tonight."

"Why?"

"Will there be alcohol there?"

"Yes, but you don't have to drink anything."

"Will there be any drugs there?"

"Not that I know of. Look, I'll protect you from all that stuff. We don't even have to stay long. We can go ride around afterwards," he said and smiled at her.

"Look, I like you, but I can't go with you tonight. I won't put myself in the position where I might be tempted to do something I shouldn't. I just can't be with you."

"Wow. You don't mess around, do you?" he said. Paige could see the hurt in his eyes and she felt like someone had punched her in the stomach. If only he knew the reason, but then again, he might feel like she was being arrogant. "Okay, fine. That's totally fine. I'm sorry I bothered you and I guess I'll see you Monday in class." Rocky turned and walked away then. Paige wanted to call out to him to come back and let her explain, but what else could she say. She didn't need to make it any worse. She quickly sent a text message to Meghan.

Need to leave.

On my way.

Meghan found Paige sitting in the passenger seat crying her eyes out. She quickly started the car and pulled out of the parking lot. She didn't say anything to her the whole way back to her house. She just let her cry. When they pulled into Paige's driveway, she finally looked up and tried to gain her composure.

"Are you going to be alright?"

"Yeah, I'll be fine."

"Listen, I know it's hard, but you made the right decision."

"Meghan, he told me I was the most amazing person he'd ever known. He asked me out on a date and I told him no. What if no one else ever asks me out again?" "What if no one ever looks at me like he did again?"

"Don't be silly. God has the right person out there for you. You just have to be patient and in his time, he will show you."

"What if I don't want anyone else but him to ask me?"

"Things will work out," Meghan encouraged.

"You're right. Thanks. I'll see you Sunday." Paige waved as Meghan drove off. Paige unlocked the door and headed straight to bed. Her thoughts were on Rocky and she prayed he hadn't stayed down at the river and done things he shouldn't have that night.

CHAPTER SIX

Rocky turned his corvette right onto the gravel road heading to the river. He was confused. He'd thought Paige was interested in him. I mean, he'd taken up for her after all. Of course, he would still take up for her even if she never went out with him. He cared about her. He didn't want anyone messing with her. That didn't help his wounded pride at the moment, though. He was disappointed she'd turned him down. No one had ever turned him down before. His ego was knocked down a notch or two. She didn't even have to think about it. It was a solid no. It was almost like she'd planned what she was going to say before he asked her.

He clicked his engine off and just sat there for a moment. He could hear the music pumping in the background. Everyone was talking and laughing. They sounded like they were having a good time, but he knew it usually ended up with people getting drunk, passing out or getting sick. Yeah, sounds like fun. NOT. He sighed as he opened his car door and got out to join the crowd.

Roman, another guy on the team, had large speakers in the back of his truck and they were blaring. When Rocky started walking toward the team, they all shouted his name. He smiled, bumped fists with a few and gave others high five.

Jake was standing off to the side talking to Kelly. She smiled up at him and flipped her hair flirtatiously. Rocky laughed out loud. She turned and smiled at Rocky.

"Oh, hey, Rocky," she said. "Is your friend okay? I hated I spilled the paint on her. I'm such a klutz."

"Yeah, I guess she's alright," Rocky replied and shrugged his shoulders. She glanced back at Jake once more and then walked away. Jake was eyeing him suspiciously.

"Looks like someone's a little interested," Rocky told Jake, nudging him in the side and motioning toward Kelly as she walked off.

"Yeah, she's cute," Jake answered, but shrugged his shoulders like he didn't care.

"That doesn't sound like it's mutual," Rocky observed.

"Not really my type," Jake responded. "Speaking of types, I thought you might bring Paige tonight. Looked like you two were getting kind of close here lately."

Rocky bitterly laughed before he answered, "Turned me down flat." Jake busted out laughing and Rocky shoved him hard, knocking him off balance. Jake caught himself before he fell and tried to pull off a straight face but failed miserably.

"Dude, I'm sorry, but this is the first time any girl has turned you down. You have to admit, it's kind of funny. You could have any girl at the school and the one you ask out tells you no. I knew I liked Paige for a reason."

Rocky rolled his eyes, but didn't comment further about his relationship status or the lack there of.

"What happened? I really thought she was interested," Jake asked trying to pry more information out of him. Before Rocky could tell him to mind his own business, Jazz stumbled over with a red solo cup in his hand. He smelled like he'd already had too much to drink.

"Rockman, you came," Jazz slurred. He threw his arm around Rocky's shoulders and spilled some of the contents of his cup on Rocky's shirt. Rocky jerked back, clearly irritated.

"Ah..man, now I'm going to smell like you do," Rocky said, irritated.

"Come on, man. That's just a party hazard. Besides, this is for you," Jazz said and handed the cup out to him. Rocky looked at it for several minutes. He knew Paige would disapprove. Why did he care what she thought though? She wouldn't go out with him. He was aggravated and needed something to take the edge off, but why did he feel so guilty about it all of the sudden. Last year, he was the party king. He could drink with the best of them and now he felt bad for even thinking about it. "Here, man." Rocky finally took the cup from Jazz's hand just as several more people walked up including Veronica and a few of her superficial friends. She locked eyes with Rocky.

"Well, I assumed Ms. Perfect would be here with you," she sneered. Her friends laughed like she'd said something funny. Rocky could feel himself getting angry. He knew he needed to play it cool, but it was going to be hard.

"It's not any of your business who comes here with me," Rocky defended.

"Like I even care, I came here with Jazz," she said

and draped herself on Jazz's arm.

"You snooze, you lose," Jazz said and laughed. Veronica and her crowd of friends laughed loudly at Jazz's comment, only showing just how much they'd all drunk that night. They were being obnoxious and it made Rocky sick.

"Yeah, have fun with all that drama," Rocky said. He turned to Jake. "I'm gone, man. See you Monday at practice." He slung the contents of the cup out and threw it in the nearby trash bag on the way back to his car. He decided right then this would be the last river party he went to. He was tired of that scene.

When he got home, he noticed the lights were still on. That meant his mom and dad were up. He really didn't want the whole "make good choices" lecture tonight, but figured it was inevitable.

He parked the car in the garage and walked in the back door, hoping to sneak upstairs without being noticed. No such luck. As soon as he opened the door his dad called out telling him to come to the kitchen.

"Hey, Mom. Hey, Dad. What's up?"

"Rocky West, you smell like beer," his mom said, giving him a pointed look. "Don't tell me you had alcohol and then got behind the wheel. I will take you down to the police station myself and have them take your license. Have we not taught you anything?"

"Mom, chill. I didn't drink anything. Jazz spilled some on me."

"What was Jazz doing with beer?" his dad asked.

"Everyone was down at the river, Dad. You know how it is," Rocky replied, trying to act all nonchalant.

"No. I don't know how it is, but I do know if the cops come down there and break up your little parties

every Friday night, you will be in serious trouble."

"Fine. Is that it? May I go to bed now?"

"Actually, this isn't the reason we called you in here," his mom told him and took a deep breath. Rocky sat down on one of the stools at the bar waiting to hear what they had to say. "Since Avery died things have changed," she started. Rocky winced. Hearing her name out loud always hit him hard. "We've decided as a family we need to start going to church and setting a better example for our children."

"Church?" Rocky asked incredulously. His mom and dad had always been the type of people who were too busy to go to church. They donated to a charity now and then and told themselves that's all they needed to do to go to Heaven.

"Yes, church. As you know, we've always believed in God, but we've never made it a point to go to church. Things need to change here. Your aunt and uncle want to go with us," she said. "I think it would be good for them. They need something to help them cope."

"What church did you have in mind?" Rocky asked. He wondered which church Paige went to and then mentally scolded himself for thinking about her. She wasn't thinking about him. He needed to stop.

"Valley Baptist. It's on the corner of Main Street. This will be good for all of us," she responded.

"Sure mom. Whatever you want to do," Rocky said and turned toward the stairs. He wanted the sanctuary of his room where he would be left alone to think things through.

"We know it's been hard on you since Avery passed away," his dad said, stopping him from making a run for the steps. Rocky shuddered. Avery was the one person who knew everything about Rocky, but still stuck by him. She was more than just his cousin/sister figure. She had always been his best friend. At least that's what he thought, but she hadn't come to him when all of this started, and that thought alone haunted him. Instead, she took her life. She didn't confide in him or ask him for help.

"Yeah, it has. I mean, I just wish I would have known what was going on with her. I hate thinking about her feeling so hopeless. She felt like that was her only option. It's just hard for me to wrap my head around," Rocky admitted. "Listen, I'm tired. I think I'll just head to bed."

"Okay, but Rocky, you know we're here if you need anything. Right?" his mom asked.

"Of course, Mom."

"Goodnight sweetie."

"Night Mom. Night Dad."

"Goodnight, son."

Rocky walked up the steps, into his bedroom and closed the door. He changed his clothes and lay down on the bed. Thoughts of Avery and Paige both filled his mind until he fell into a restless sleep.

Paige stayed in on Saturday. She was sad. Her mom wanted to get some housework done, so Paige started cleaning as hard as she could. She tried to use that to keep her mind off of Rocky, but it didn't help. She continued to see the forlorn look on his face when she'd said no. It just broke her heart every time she thought about it. With everything in her, she wanted to say yes to him. She wanted to go out with him. She wanted to be his girl, but knew she couldn't. Why did things like this have to be so complicated? Why couldn't he go to church, be a Christian and be serious about serving God? Why did she have to fall for him in the first place? Yes, if Paige was being honest with herself, she really liked Rocky West.

All day Saturday, she worked as hard as she could. She also prayed as hard as she could. She prayed God would help her through this. She prayed God would show her what to do and give her some peace.

Sunday morning, Paige was feeling much better about everything. She was still sad and hadn't gotten over Rocky, but she knew God would help her through it. She hurried to get ready, taking a little extra time fixing her hair and makeup. She was singing a solo with the youth choir this morning. She was a little nervous about it and wanted to look her best. She picked out a yellow sundress. It came just below her knees. It was sleeveless. It was one of her favorites. She put her pearl earrings in her ears and headed downstairs to grab breakfast before church.

"Good morning, sweetheart," Ellen said to Paige as she walked in the kitchen. "I've fixed your favorite."

"Thanks, Mom." Paige sat down at the kitchen table while her mom brought her a plate of French toast and syrup. "You're the best."

"Nothing but the best for my girl."

"Um, Mom, I was wondering if you'd like to come to church with me this morning," Paige asked, nervously. "I'm singing a solo."

"Sweetie, you know church just isn't for me anymore. That's over and done with. I don't try to make you stay at home, so don't try and make me go."

"Mom, please," Paige urged. Ellen looked at her daughter for a moment before answering.

"Tell you what. When you come home, we'll go do something together. Something fun. What about a nice hike? We haven't done that in ages."

Paige couldn't keep the disappointment from showing, "Sure, Mom."

"There's my good girl. You go and have fun and I'll see you when you get back." How many times had Paige asked her mom to go to church? Her mom was angry with God. Ellen felt like God could have prevented her dad's heart attack. She thought God should have saved his life. They were a family that never missed a service before he'd had his heart attack and died. He didn't even make it to the hospital that night. They didn't get a chance to say goodbye or tell him how much they loved him one last time. Ever since the tragedy that changed their lives forever, Ellen hadn't stepped a foot back in the church. The pastor and several members had come to see her and talk to her, but she wouldn't hear it. She never discouraged Paige from going, but she just wouldn't go with her.

Paige finished her breakfast, brushed her teeth and slipped her white sandals on before telling her mom bye.

"I'm gone, Mom," Paige shouted.

"Okay, sweets. Hurry home and good luck today," Ellen told her daughter.

"Thanks, mom," Paige replied. She couldn't help but fell disappointed her mom hadn't decided to come with her. It would have been nice to know her mom was sitting out in the pew supporting her.

Paige drove to church without listening to the radio.

She hummed her solo and went over the words again and again in her head. She would hate to get up there and forget them.

When she entered the building, she saw Meghan. She waved her over and Paige followed.

"You look scared to death," Meghan teased.

"You know how much I hate getting up in front of people," Paige said.

"You'll be fine. What about your Mom? Did she come?"

"No, she wouldn't. It breaks my heart, Meghan."

"We'll just keep praying. She'll come back." Meghan hugged her best friend and they headed downstairs for Sunday school.

After Sunday school was over, they came back upstairs for the worship service. It was time for the youth choir to sing. Paige's hands were sweating and she felt like something was stuck in her throat as she followed everyone up on stage. Monica, the youth leader, handed her the microphone and sat down at the piano.

Paige sucked in a deep breath and looked out at the crowd. Most of the time, she looked just above their heads, but for some reason, she didn't this time and then she locked eyes with Rocky West. He was sitting on the back pew of the church. Paige felt like someone had hit her in the stomach. He was looking right back at her, but his face was void of any emotion. She was sure her emotions were written all over her. She didn't even hear the piano begin to play and totally missed her cue to start the song. Meghan nudged her.

Paige looked over at Monica and she smiled and nodded. Paige turned back toward the crowd again. He was still staring right at her, but then he did something she didn't expect. He smiled and nodded his head. There he was, giving her just enough encouragement to start her song. Paige began to sing and then the youth choir came in on the chorus. She didn't look away from him the entire song. She couldn't. There was just something about the way he looked at her. It made her feel special.

When the song was over, the entire congregation clapped for them. Everyone made their way to their seats as the Pastor stood for the sermon.

"What was up with you?" Meghan whispered.

"Rocky is here." Paige whispered back, feeling all flustered again.

"WHAT?" Meghan said, way too loud. Several of the adults gave them stern looks. Paige wanted to crawl under the pew and she gave Meghan a look as well.

"Don't turn around. He's sitting on the back pew, but don't.." Paige whispered, but Meghan looked toward the back. "I can't believe you just turned around."

"Interesting," Meghan said and smiled. "He's looking over here."

"What is interesting about that?" Paige asked. "He probably thinks I'm crazy."

"He may not be a lost cause just yet," she said and then turned her attention to their Pastor.

Secretly, Paige wished that were true with all her heart. She put her faith in God that he knew best and he wouldn't lead her on the wrong path.

After the service was over, she felt like she should say something to him. She made her way up the side of the pews and out the back door. She saw him standing by himself, while his parents spoke with the pastor.

He had on a light blue polo shirt and khaki pants. He looked handsome standing there in the sun. He hadn't noticed her walk up.

"Rocky?" she said, tentatively.

"Oh, hey, Paige. I have to say. I'm impressed. You have a beautiful voice," he said. He sounded so sincere at the moment. It made Paige blush. He smiled at her and Paige felt like her insides melted.

"You don't have to say that," she replied.

"It's the truth," he said. They stood in awkward silence for a moment. "Look, I'm sorry about Friday night. I was way out of line asking you out."

"You were?" Paige asked, surprised he'd brought it up.

"Yeah. Look, we were just getting to be friends and here I try to mess things up. I've had a day to think about it and I realized I was a jerk."

"No, not at all."

"Can we just be friends again and forget I did that?" he asked. Paige hated the way she felt at the moment. Her stomach dropped, but she plastered a smile on her face.

"Friends," she said and stuck her hand out to shake his. He took her hand in his and he held a moment longer than she expected.

"Great. I guess I'll see you in class tomorrow, friend," he said, putting his emphasis on the word friend.

"See you then," Paige answered. He walked off toward his parents, only turning around once to throw her another smile. She watched as he walked to the car and got in. Then, his parents pulled out of the parking lot.

"Earth to Paige," Meghan said, coming to stand beside her. She was just standing there looking at the empty parking place.

"He just wants to be friends," Paige said quietly, more to herself than anyone.

"Well, that's good news, right? At least he's not mad at you for turning him down. Everything will work out the way it's supposed to. Have faith."

"Yeah, I guess you're right," Paige answered. She went back in the church, gathered her stuff up and headed home. She should be thankful he still wanted to be her friend. Instead, she just felt horrible and she didn't know why.

CHAPTER SEVEN

Paige and Rocky fell into a routine of sorts. They talked every day, even on Saturdays and Sundays, even if it was only through text or messenger. He looked out for her all he could while he was at school and even started helping her a little in history with her assignments. She answered all the questions he was having about church and the bible. Rocky found the more he listened at church on Sunday mornings the more he wanted to know. Paige was very patient with him and helped him all she could.

She'd also been to every game of the season so far. She brought Meghan, and a few more girls from the church had started coming with her and they sat on the bleachers and cheered for the team. It made Rocky happy knowing she was there. He played harder than he ever had and it paid off. They hadn't lost a game yet. They saw each other every day at school and on Sundays. He thought the effect she had on him might wear off, but she still got to him every day. In fact, it was getting worse. The more he saw her and got to know the real Paige, the more he wanted to know. She was quickly becoming one of the most important things in his life.

Friday evening, Meghan stopped by his locker. "Hey, Rocky." She looked like a girl on a mission.

"Hey, Meghan. Is everyone coming to the game?" Rocky asked, knowing they would.

"Oh yeah. We haven't missed one all season. Paige is really getting into them here lately," Meghan said. Rocky smiled to himself as he finished putting his books in his locker. He wished Paige would be interested in him instead of the game. He'd told her they would be friends and she was becoming his best friend. Still, he couldn't help but notice the way her eyes lit up when she teased him or how caring she was to everyone around. He noticed how her silky, brown hair was just the right length to fall over her shoulders when it was down and her eyes were like looking at emeralds shining at him. She was a gentle soul and he wanted to be the one who made her feel special. Instead, he pretended he only wanted to be friends. At least he wouldn't totally lose her that way. If he pursued a relationship, she might cut him off completely and he couldn't have that.

"Anyhow, Paige's birthday is next week."

"What day?" he asked and turned around to look at her. He was mentally kicking himself for not knowing her birthday was coming up. What kind of friend was he?

"Next Thursday. I'm throwing her a little surprise party that evening. It's just some friends from church and her mom. I thought you might like to come," Meghan said. She looked a little unsure of what he would say.

"Yeah, definitely. When and where?" he asked. This was Paige's birthday. He wouldn't miss it for anything.

"The Pizza Shack. Thursday evening at 7."

"What does she like? I mean, what can I get her?"

"You'll figure it out," Meghan said and walked off leaving him staring after her. She'd confused him. Figure it out? He had no idea what to get her. Paige wasn't your normal girl. She didn't seem like the type that would like all the stuff that the superficial girls he'd been around would like. He wondered if she even liked flowers, but didn't all girls like roses?

He turned around and saw Veronica watching him. She looked angry again and he wondered if she was ever happy. He sighed and headed to the gym, completely ignoring her. He had to get ready for the game.

Paige had only been home from the game about ten minutes when her phone went off. She had a text message. She smiled knowing it would be Rocky. Her heart fluttered in her chest.

Thx for coming tonight.

YW I'm your biggest fan ▢

She smiled again. He always told her thank you. She'd actually gotten really interested in football, but it gave her another excuse to be around Rocky. Meghan told her she was falling for him and she denied it, but deep down, she knew it was true. She needed to distance herself from him, but it was becoming harder and harder to do.

She snuggled down in bed with her latest book when her phone went off again. She jumped up. She assumed it would be Rocky. She got back under the covers and pulled up her messages.

What do you get a loser for their birthday? V

Paige didn't know how Veronica had gotten her number, but that's the only person she knew who was called V. The message bothered her. She quickly deleted it and tried to put it out of her mind. Maybe it was an accident and she wasn't actually harassing her. Then, it went off again. Her stomach dropped.

Happy birthday to you. Happy birthday to you. You act like your perfect, but we all know the truth.

Tears stung the back of her eyes and she quickly deleted the message. Her first thought was to call Rocky. He would put a stop to this, but she knew he and Jazz were barely speaking and she felt like it was her fault. Jazz was Veronica's boyfriend now and Paige didn't want to cause any hard feelings between Rocky and his friend.

So, she pulled up the message again and blocked her number. She would just have to stop this on her own. She wasn't perfect at all. She'd never pretended to be, but the words stung. She didn't know why Veronica was always so mean to her.

She sat her phone on her nightstand and quickly turned off the lamp. She didn't feel like reading anymore. All she wanted to do was to forget about what the message said. When her phone buzzed again, she cringed. She almost didn't look, but she picked it up telling herself she'd already blocked Veronica's number.

Goodnight, pretty girl.

It was Rocky. She did cry then. He was the most

caring guy she'd ever known. She quickly swiped a response back to him.

Night, Rocky. See you Sunday??

I'll be there. Sit with me?

Sure.

TTYL.

Even when he wasn't trying, he made everything better. He would be furious if he knew Veronica had gotten her number and messaged her. She just wouldn't say anything. She would take care of it herself. She had to.

Thursday evening, Rocky was at home getting ready for Paige's party. There was a knock on his bedroom door. He shouted for the person to come in. He was surprised to see Jazz.

"Hey, man," Jazz said.

"Jazz, what's up?"

"I've been feeling like things are messed up. I'm with Veronica now and you're practically with the Christian girl."

"The Christian girl has a name," Rocky said, feeling irritated he'd referred to Paige that way.

"Fine, you're with Paige."

"I'm not with Paige. We're just friends," Rocky argued.

"You've totally changed for this girl. You might not be official, but you're with her," Jazz said. "I don't understand you. It's like we weren't ever friends."

"I'm just laying low. I don't like the way Veronica

treats Paige."

"Yeah, I know. I've actually talked to her about it," Jazz said.

"Really?"

"Yeah. I told her to lay off."

"Thanks man. I appreciate that. Maybe she'll listen to you."

"Where are you going?"

"It's Paige's birthday. They are having a small get together for her. It's a surprise."

"Mind if I tag along?"

"You don't want to do that," Rocky said. He knew Meghan would be furious if he brought Jazz with him. He didn't want Paige uncomfortable at her own party either.

"I won't cause any trouble. Besides, it will give me a chance to apologize to her in person and tell her things are going to change."

"Jazz, you don't exactly roll with the people they do," Rocky argued again.

"You're seriously telling me no?" Jazz said. "I'm asking to come to this party to apologize to your girl."

"Fine, you can come. I better not regret this," Rocky warned.

"No worries. Everything's great," Jazz said and flashed him one of his infamous smiles. Rocky rolled his eyes and told him to come on.

They drove to the Pizza Shack and went in. It was closed to customers for the private party. Meghan worked there so she'd reserved the entire place. She turned around to see him and Jazz entering. Yep, he was right. She was furious.

"Rocky West, may I speak to you? ALONE," she

said and stormed off.

"Yeah, I'm heading over there," Jazz said, pointing in the opposite direction. He walked off leaving Rocky with a livid Meghan.

"What were you thinking bringing him to Paige's party?"

"He asked to come. He wants to apologize to her for being mean to her. I thought that might be nice on her birthday. See, it's not as bad as you think. Chill," Rocky said.

"He better not get out of line, Rocky."

"I'm responsible for him. He won't."

Just then, Paige walked in with her mom and everyone yelled surprise. She jumped and everyone laughed at the startled expression on her face. Abby and Kaylee ran up to her and hugged her. Rocky held back and let her friends have their time.

"Meghan, what have you done?" she asked. Meghan just laughed and hugged her.

"Happy birthday, Paige," she said. Everyone was going up to Paige wishing her happy birthday. Rocky hung back with Jazz until she looked at him and smiled. Her smile died quickly as she looked at Jazz. Rocky quickly walked up to her. He wanted to explain why Jazz was there before she jumped to the wrong conclusion.

"Rocky?" she asked in a hesitant voice and glanced at Jazz again.

"It's okay. I think you'll be glad he's here," Rocky said. He motioned for Jazz.

"Hey, Paige. Look, I've never really given you a reason to like me or think I'm anything but a jerk. I just wanted to tell you I'm sorry for the way I treated you.

Can we maybe start over and be friends?"

Paige hesitated before speaking. "Sure." Rocky released the breath he'd been holding.

"Happy birthday, pretty girl," Rocky said, giving her his full attention. She grinned and blushed.

"That's my cue to leave," Jazz said and winked at her.

"Is he serious?" Paige asked when he couldn't hear her.

"I think so. He just showed up at my house wanting to talk. He asked me where I was going and I told him. He asked if he could come and apologize to you. You're always seeing the good in people. I thought you'd be glad. Are you glad?"

"I am. It's just a one eighty turn around from the way he usually is." Rocky had to agree. He wondered what brought it on, but didn't voice his thoughts to Paige.

She mingled with the rest of the people who'd come to her party. Rocky held back, just watching her. Everyone ate pizza and was having a great time, laughing and talking. Meghan declared it was time for cake. She went to the back to get the cake and brought it out. It was still in the box when she sat it down on the table.

"Paige, you are going to love it." She opened the box and it slipped from her hands and hit the table. The layers on the cake shifted but Paige could still see what the words said. Happy Birthday Loser. Tears came to her eyes. "Oh my gosh. Paige, I'm so sorry. This isn't your cake. Your cake was beautiful. How could this happen?"

The bells rang as the front door opened and in walked Veronica, Molly and Kelly.

"This is a private party," Meghan said, when she saw

the mean girls.

"But we brought the cake," Veronica said and laughed. She walked over to Jazz and he threw his arm around her. "Hey, baby."

"You knew she was going to do this?" Rocky accused.

"Of course. Tell me you didn't believe the whole give me another chance bull, did you?"

"Young man, you need to leave this place immediately," Ellen spoke up and said.

"Oh, don't worry. We're not staying," Veronica said. "I just came here to give sweet, little Paige her birthday gift."

"I don't want anything you have to offer," Paige said.

"Oh, you'll want to know this. Remember last year when you planned your prayer around the pole meetings every Wednesday morning?"

"Yes," Paige said, looking very confused. Rocky stiffened. He knew exactly what was coming.

"Veronica, you and your so called friends need to get out of here," Rocky warned. He moved to stand in front of Paige and was giving Veronica and Jazz a threatening look.

"What's wrong, Rocky? Afraid your little girlfriend won't like the truth?"

"Shut up, Veronica," he threatened. "I mean it. Get out of here." He was furious. Of all times to bring this up, she had to do it now. Paige would be so upset with him.

"Rocky, what's this about?" Paige asked and touched his arm. Ellen moved closer to Paige as well.

"Here little girl, let me tell you," Veronica began. "We all saw the flyers you posted up everywhere in school. We didn't plan on going, but your little boyfriend Rocky decided to take matters into his own hands. He snuck in the maintenance office and changed the times for the sprinklers to cut on. Then, he was the one who stood and watched as all of you got soaking wet and snapped the pictures and posted them on online. He laughed for weeks about that. Every time you tried to have a meeting, he would make sure those sprinklers went off until you finally gave up. That's the guy who's taking up for you now and being your knight in shining armor."

"That's enough, Veronica. Get out of here," Rocky said through clenched teeth. Jazz stood up and Rocky punched him straight in the face. "You're dead to me, man. You hear me. You're nothing to me." Paige and Meghan both screamed. "Get out of here. I won't tell you again."

"Fine, we're gone, but the damage is done. Oh yeah, happy birthday, Paige," Veronica said. Jazz got up and wiped blood from his nose where Rocky had hit him. They eyed each other, but Jazz backed down. Rocky stood there, breathing hard, waiting for them to go. He turned to look at Paige and silent tears were coming down her face.

"It was you?" she asked.

"Listen, it was last year. I wasn't the same person I am now. I didn't mean anything by it. It was a stupid prank. I wish I could take it back, but I can't. I'm sorry you found out like this."

"Meghan, let's get this stuff cleaned up," Ellen said. "I think the party is over everyone." Paige just stood there as everyone told her bye and wished her happy birthday again. Unfortunately, this wasn't going to be a happy birthday. Ellen and Meghan disappeared to the kitchen, leaving Rocky alone with Paige after the others left. She wouldn't even look at him.

"Come on. You know I've changed," Rocky started and Paige turned to him. He saw the despair in her eyes.

"You don't know what kind of courage it took for me to try and start a group like that. I'm not good in front of people, but I really wanted it to be a good thing. Every week, the crowd got fewer and fewer because people wouldn't chance getting wet. The last week I was there, I was completely alone. I don't think I'd ever felt as alone as I did that day. Now, I find out you were behind that all the time. What am I supposed to do with that?"

"Forgive me, please Paige. Look, I'm sorry. I was just being stupid."

"Oh no. You don't get off that easy. That was cruel, not stupid." Ellen and Meghan walked out of the kitchen.

"Everything's cleaned up now sweetie. Are you ready to go home?" Ellen asked.

"Yeah, mom."

"Let's load your presents in the car. Maybe you'll feel like opening them later," she encouraged. Paige nodded her head and followed her mom outside. Rocky stood there watching her as she sat in the passenger seat. Her mom drove away and Rocky knew this was bad. He felt like he'd just lost part of himself. He grabbed his phone out of his pocket and sent her a text.

Please forgive me.

Leave me alone.

His heart felt like someone had stabbed it with a knife. She told him to leave her alone. No, he couldn't do that. He was losing his best friend. He was losing the girl he loved. Wait, what? He loved her? Yes, he realized he loved her. He had to fix this.

"Jerk," Meghan said as she slapped the back of his head.

"Ow," he replied, but didn't argue with her. He deserved that and a lot more.

"You just let her walk out," Meghan said. "You better find some way to fix this."

"I will. I have to."

"Go home, Rocky."

"See you around, Meghan," he answered.

"Yeah, maybe," she replied. He quickly walked to his car and got in the driver's seat. He pulled his phone out and sent another message to her.

You asked me to leave you alone. I can't. I won't. You're too important to me. I'll find a way to make this up to you. I'll show you I'm worth forgiving. I don't want to lose you, Paige. Not now, not ever.

He waited for a reply, but none came. He started his Corvette and drove home slowly. He had to figure this out and he would get even with Veronica and Jazz if it was the last thing he did.

CHAPTER EIGHT

Paige cried herself to sleep that night and woke up with a terrible headache. Her mom came in her room and sat down on the bed when her alarm clock started going off and she didn't immediately get up.

"How are you, sweetie?" Ellen asked, as she brushed her hair out of her face. Paige started to cry again. "Come now. You're stronger than this. You've faced a lot of persecution for being a Christian before. Why does this bother you so bad? It's because of Rocky, isn't it? You've fallen for him."

"I know I shouldn't have, Mom. He asked me out and I told him no because I know he's not saved and the bible is plain about being unequally yoked, but sometimes he's just so wonderful. He made me feel like I was important. I know he's changed from last year. Things are different, but I'm not sure I'll get passed this. I felt like such a failure last year and now I know he was behind it. How do I forgive him for that?"

"Well, I'm furious with him, but I know you and you'll find it in your heart to forgive him. You're too good of a person not to."

"Mom, I don't think I can face everyone today. Can I stay home?"

"Paige Jones, you've never run from anything in your life."

"I'm not running. I just need a little more time to get myself together. I can't go in there and face everyone with my face swollen from crying and my eyes red and bloodshot. I can't let them see that."

"Fine, I'll call the school and tell them you won't be there today. We are not making a habit of this young lady. Next week, I expect you there every day."

"Thanks, Mom." Ellen hugged her daughter and then left her alone again. She snuggled back under the covers, planning to take full advantage of a day at home. She quickly texted Meghan to tell her she was staying home so she wouldn't be worried. She pulled up Rocky's last text and read it again. He said he didn't want to lose her, but it was too late. She couldn't look at him the same. She quickly closed her eyes wanting sleep to come again. Her phone went off and she figured it was Meghan answering her back.

R U up? We need to talk. You have to let me explain.

Paige cringed when she saw it was from Rocky. She read it, though. She pulled up his contact information and told herself to delete the messages and block his number. At least then she wouldn't have to torture herself each time he tried to call or text her. She stared at her phone a few seconds. She wasn't ready to do that yet. It was going to take her some time to be ready to delete him from her life.

U there?

Not feeling well today. Won't be at school.

She knew she shouldn't have answered him, but she didn't want him to continue to text her all day. She just hoped it wouldn't encourage him to talk to her more. Talking to Rocky West was the last thing she wanted to do right now if ever again.

Feel better. TTYL.

She felt like crying again. Her heart was broken into a million pieces and she knew only the Lord would be able to put her back together. She got out of the bed and knelt down on the floor.

"Dear Heavenly Father, please help me as I try to deal with this. I feel so heart broken and I know you can help me through. I had placed trust and confidence in him when I should have looked to you. Please forgive me for losing sight of what's truly important. Heal my heart, Lord. Only you can. Thank you for everything you've done for me, but most of all for your grace and mercy. Amen."

Paige felt better already. She climbed back into bed, slid beneath the covers and went to sleep. She needed some rest and a break from reality at the moment. A heart could only take so much before there was no coming back from the hurt. She didn't wake up until 3 pm that afternoon and she felt refreshed. She hesitantly looked at her phone, but there were only the messages she'd received was from Meghan, Abby and Kaylee telling her they would be over later for a sleep over. She was glad Rocky hadn't sent her anything else. Maybe

he'd finally gotten the message that she didn't want
anything else to do with him.

Jake had stayed with Rocky most of the day. He'd
heard what happened at Paige's party and knew Rocky
would be itching for a fight. They both walked in the
boys' locker room and Jazz turned to look at them. Jazz
had a bandage on his nose. Rocky stood and stared at
Jazz until Jake nudged him to go on.

Rocky went to his locker and got ready for the game.
The coach came in and gave them a speech about scoring
another victory. The team shouted in approval. At least
everyone on the team did but Rocky and Jazz. They
continued their stare down from opposite sides of the
locker room. There was an underlying tension in the
room and everybody seemed to be a little more on edge.

Once out on the field, Rocky couldn't help but look
for Paige. He knew she wouldn't be there, but it was
habit. He felt so horrible for hurting her like that. He
just needed to talk to her and try to explain things.
Maybe she could understand and forgive him, but she at
least she needed to hear his side.

Their team had the ball first and once it was kicked
off and returned, Rocky got into position. He called the
play. One minute he was ready to throw the ball and the
next minute he was lying on his back. This was the first
time he'd been sacked all year. The defense hadn't let
anyone through the line before this game. The opposing
team's crowd was going crazy for a moment. The hit had
knocked the breath out of him. He lay there not moving
and the crowd eventually grew quiet. Jake and Roman

came to kneel beside him. His coach and assistant coach came out on the field to check him as well.

"You okay, son?" Coach asked.

"Sure, coach," Rocky replied. They helped him stand up and he shook it off. His side hurt a little, but other than that, he was fine. That's when he looked up into the smug face of Jazz. He should have known he was the one who'd let the guy through. He was in full on rage mode, but Jake got in front of him. Rocky saw red and all he could think about was knocking Jazz into next week.

"Shake it off. We'll deal with it later," he said to Rocky. Rocky nodded his head and got back into position.

Second down. Rocky was ready to get this show on the road. He called the play and just like before, Jazz let the guy through. Rocky was ready this time, though and dodged him. He tossed the ball to his receiver before getting knocked down this time. He stood back up again and grabbed Jazz by the facemask. The referee blew the whistle and threw up a flag.

"Let go of me, Rocky," Jazz screamed.

"You do that again and I'll have Coach take you out of the game," Rocky threatened.

"Whatever," Jazz replied, and shoved Rocky as hard as he could.

"Try me," Rocky said. He shoved Jazz back. The ref penalized them ten yards. Rocky took one look over at their coach and knew he was angry with them. He told himself he had to get his head back in the game.

Third down. Rocky was shaken up. This time, when he threw the ball it was intercepted and the other team ran it all the way back for a touchdown. Rocky felt defeated as the coach motioned them off the field for a timeout.

When the game ended, they'd lost 7 to 0. They hadn't scored one single point. The team was quiet as the Coach raked them over the coals about everything they did wrong. When he was finished screaming at the team, he told Rocky and Jazz to get in his office and wait for him.

They both did as they were told. "This is your fault," Jazz said with his arms crossed over his chest.

"Seriously? You were the one letting people through the line," Rocky accused.

"No, you started this when you forgot who your real friends were," Jazz answered.

"You're pathetic. Maybe I just didn't like the way my so called friends were treating other people."

They both got quiet again as the Coach walked in and slammed the door. He eyed both of them as he sat down behind his desk.

"Who wants to tell me what's going on with you two?" They both remained silent. "Okay, so no one wants to tell me." Rocky and Jazz both looked at each other but didn't speak. "Fine then. When you two yahoos decide to tell me, we'll talk. Until then, be ready for some extra practices. The team is scheduled to be here at six in the morning. You two will be here at five or you're off the team. Both of you. I want you to run suicides until your team shows up. Oh don't worry; I'll be here to make sure you're doing it. You're also on cleanup duty. You will scrub every locker, shower, floor, sink and mirror in this locker room. I will expect it to be shining come Monday morning. Any questions?"

"No sir," they mumbled, clearly irritated.

"Oh come on, guys, you can do better than that," he

said.

"No sir," they both said a little louder.

"Alright. See you bright and early in the morning, girls," he said as he taunted them and motioned to the door. They both got up and walked out. Jazz slammed his own locker shut and headed outside.

"What was all that about?" Jake asked Rocky.

"We're being punished because Coach knows something's up with me and Jazz," Rocky explained.

"Well, at least it might take your mind off Paige," Jake said as they walked out of the locker room.

"If only," Rocky said.

"Are you going to call her tonight?"

"I don't know."

"I'll see you in the morning, man," Jake said, as he held up his fist for Rocky to bump it. Then, he walked off toward his car.

"Yeah, see ya." Rocky got in his corvette, revved the engine and turned his radio on as loud as he could take it. He spun out of the parking lot and headed home. Once he got there and went inside, he slipped upstairs without his parents even knowing. He pulled his phone out and pulled up Paige's number. He held his thumb over the call button for several seconds before shutting it back off and placing it on his nightstand. He just wasn't in the frame of mind he needed to be in when he talked to Paige.

Paige was happy when Meghan called that afternoon. She declared that she, Abby and Kaylee were coming over for a sleepover. They needed some girl time. When six o'clock rolled around, they did all the girl things they could.

Ellen ordered pizza for all of them. They quickly got into their pajamas. They did makeovers and watched movies. They popped some popcorn and did each other's nails. Paige was feeling a lot better. Just being around her friends, people who truly cared about her, was helping so much. They even took some time for a devotional.

Paige got her bible out and read, "Therefore I take pleasure in infirmities, in reproaches, in necessities, in persecutions, in distresses for Christ's sake, for when I am weak, then am I strong. 2 Corinthians 12:10. I woke up this afternoon and pulled my bible out. This scripture just popped out to me. I was heartbroken all over again yesterday evening, but this scripture made me feel better." Abby came over and gave her a hug.

"Paige, you are such an amazing person," she encouraged.

"No, I'm not," Paige argued.

"You know you are," Meghan said as she threw a pillow at her and hit her in the head. That started the pillow fight war of the century. They were hitting each other with pillows, screaming and laughing. Paige felt like a weight had been lifted off her shoulders again. Some pizza, movies, a pillow fight and girl time was exactly what the doctor had ordered for her to lift her spirits.

Kaylee's phone beeped. "Hey, guys. Let's call a truce so I can check my phone."

"Fine, but if you quit, you forfeit," Meghan said.

Kaylee laughed, but she threw her hands up and

grabbed her phone from her bag. "Oh my goodness." Everyone stopped and looked at Kaylee.

"Is something wrong?" Paige asked.

"No," Kaylee said, but they could tell something was wrong.

"What it is, Kay?" Abby said.

"I'm afraid Paige doesn't want to hear about it," she answered.

"What?" Paige asked.

"I asked a girl in my class to text me and tell me how the game went. I've really gotten interested in football and I was just curious."

Paige could feel the anxiety rising up in her again. The last thing she wanted to hear about was how well Rocky played or how much they beat the other team. Instead, she plastered a smile that would have made the best actress be envious and told her to tell them what was going on.

"They lost," Kaylee answered. "This is the first game all season."

"Whoa, I can't believe it," Meghan answered. "They've been on a roll." She was giving Paige a knowing look.

"But you haven't heard the worst part," Kaylee responded. "Rocky got sacked more than one time tonight."

"Is he hurt?" Paige asked, her voice betraying her because it was filled with so much concern. Meghan gave her another look, but she just wanted to throw a pillow at her best friend and tell her to shut it.

"The girl said the first time he was knocked down he didn't get up for a while. He finished the game, but something was wrong with him," Kaylee said. "I know you're mad at him Paige, but I thought you might like to know that."

"Thank you, Kaylee. I might be a little mad at him, but I don't want anything to happen to him," Paige answered. "I think I'll head downstairs and get us some more drinks. Who wants a bottle of water?"

"I do," Kaylee said.

"Me," Abby responded.

"I'll go help you," Meghan said and followed her out the bedroom door.

"I'm fine Meghan, you don't have to come down here and pretend to help me so you can make sure I'm okay," Paige said after they made it to the kitchen.

"It's okay not to want him to be hurt. You care about him. Yeah, I know he hurt you. I saw how upset you were when you finally cancelled the prayer around the pole last year. To find out the guy you have a thing for was behind it, well, that stinks. I know you, though. I'm sure you're worried about him. Why don't you see if he's alright?"

"No. I can't talk to him."

"I think you'll feel better if you do," Meghan suggested. "Do you want to know why his head wasn't in the game?"

"He was hurt," Paige said matter of fact.

"No. He knew you weren't there. He knows things between you guys are not good and he couldn't concentrate on playing because he was worried about you. Listen, I saw him today at school. I didn't talk to him. I basically dodged him anyway I could, but he was clearly upset. Jake was walking with him the entire day like some kind of bull dog protecting his owner."

"If I call him, he'll think things are okay with us, and

they're not."

"I'll take the water upstairs. You decide. I won't judge you no matter what your decision is." Paige just nodded at Meghan as she walked back upstairs. Just then, her phone buzzed. She knew who it was before she even looked to see. She pulled it out of her pocket.

Hey.

Before she could talk herself out of it, she called him. He answered on the first ring.

"Paige?" he said. He sounded very surprised.

"Hey," she said. After that, she didn't know what to say. She drew a blank for a
moment and started mindlessly fidgeting with the edge of her tank top.

"I'm glad you called. I wasn't sure if you would ever call me again," he said. Paige let out a long breath.

"I heard you got hurt tonight. I wanted to make sure you were okay," she said.

"Really? You cared enough about me to check on me?"

"Look, Rocky. I'm mad at you. No, I'm livid, but I don't want you hurt."

"I'm okay. I got sacked a few times. The first time I wasn't expecting it. It knocked the breath out of me and I'm pretty sure my ribs are bruised, but I'll be fine. Well, at least I will be until tomorrow."

"What's happening tomorrow?" Paige asked. She sounded worried about him again. She could kick herself.

"Well, because we lost we have practice tomorrow. Jazz and I have to be there an hour early to run suicides. Then after practice, we have to clean the locker room."

"Wow. Doesn't sound like much fun to me," she

said. Paige started to get nervous. She wasn't falling back to being friendly with him yet. "Well, I just wanted to make sure you were okay. I'll talk to you sometime."

"Paige?" he said, right before she hung up.

"Yeah?"

"Please, may I come over and just explain some stuff to you."

"Look, it's late and I have people here," she started.

"What about tomorrow after practice?"

She hesitated. She knew this might be for the best. They could get everything out in the open. "Fine. Text me before you come."

"Okay. I will. Thanks Paige."

"See ya, Rocky," she said and hung up the phone. She stared at it a few more minutes before she headed back upstairs. When she got back in there, Meghan had put on some music and they were doing really bad impressions of Elvis Presley. Paige started laughing. She felt better. Rocky was okay. She was going to talk to him and tell him how she felt. Things would be okay. Just before she joined in on the worst dancing in the history of all dancing, her phone buzzed. She looked down.

Night, pretty girl.

She sighed and put her phone up without answering him.

CHAPTER NINE

Rocky was at the field at 4:50 a.m. impatiently waiting on Jazz and the Coach to get there. He was ready to get this day over with so he could see Paige and clear the air. She'd cared enough about him to call and check on him last night and that thought alone made him happy and helped him get up early that morning and go to practice. He hoped just maybe he could still save their friendship. He was afraid to let himself hope for any more than that.

Jazz walked in looking mostly asleep with his ruffled hair and tired eyes. If they hadn't been in such a bad place where their friendship was concerned, Rocky might have cracked a joke about him looking like the walking dead or something similar to it. Instead, he tried his best to ignore him, but one thing Rocky couldn't ignore was the tension igniting between them. Jazz was totally okay with being ignored. He was sipping on some coffee and staring at the ground or anywhere but at Rocky.

Coach walked in, all smiles. "Alright you pansies, you're going to run from the ten yard line to the forty yard line and back twice in 30 seconds or you are going to do it again. You're going to keep doing it until you make it."

"That's not possible," Rocky said, sounding

outraged.

"Well, then I guess you'll run for an hour, quarterback. You got a problem with that?" Coach asked in an intimidating way that told them they better not have a problem with it.

"No sir," Rocky answered. Jazz mumbled something and glanced at him with an irritated look. "What was that?"

"I said, learn to keep your trap shut," Jazz growled in reply.

"Learn to mind your own business," Rocky threw back at him. They walked up to the ten-yard line and waited for the coach to blow the whistle.

"Eat my dust, lover boy," Jazz taunted.

"Bite me, loser," Rocky answered back. If he hadn't been so mad at him, he would have cracked a smile. For the next hour, they ran suicide drills non-stop. By the time the rest of the team got there, Rocky and Jazz were laying across the ten-yard line, gasping for breath.

"Looks like you two are beat," Jake said and chuckled a little to himself.

"Nah, these two are just getting warmed up," Coach said. "Roman, start the warm up stretches. I think Rocky can use a breather."

"Sure thing, Coach," Roman responded and the other team members started their normal warm up routine.

"I guess you pansies need to get up and start acting like team members again or we'll be here next Saturday," Coach threatened.

"Yes, Coach," they mumbled.

"What was that?" he said.

"Yes, Coach," they both responded louder.

"Good. Now, have about a five-minute break and

then join your team. The torture isn't over yet."

"Look man, let's just call a truce already so we can get back to football," Rocky said.

"I'll call a truce when you dump little Ms. Perfect and come back to your real friends. Seriously, do you even wonder how I'm getting to school now? You quit picking me up and you never even said anything to me about it. What kind of friend does that?"

"Dude, we aren't speaking. I'm not picking you up and last I checked you have a license and a car. You're not helpless. I'm not with Paige. Do I want to be? Yes, but thanks to you and Veronica that probably won't happen."

"If you're looking for an apology, you're not going to get it," Jazz said. "You don't belong with her. She doesn't belong in our world." That infuriated Rocky, but he just stared at Jazz. There was no point in arguing with him.

"Well, at least play the game right. Quit letting guys through the line just because you're trying to get even with me. That's pretty lame and we'll end up here every Saturday if you keep it up," Rocky said.

"I'll do my job on the field, but that's the only place I have your back," Jazz said. He walked off from him then. Rocky rolled his eyes, but joined the team. They were doing some stretches before Roman started in on the drills. He was glad someone else was taking the lead this morning. He just wanted to get this practice over with and clean the locker room so he could see Paige. They had a lot to talk about and he was anxious to get it over with.

Paige stared at herself in the mirror. She'd worn her brown hair down. She flat ironed it and it looked very smooth and sleek. She fussed with her clothes a little more than necessary. She told herself not to get worked up about him coming over, but she couldn't help it. She still wanted to look good, even if she was furious with him and didn't know if they would be able to repair their friendship. She didn't understand herself or her thoughts. She hated the fact that she was secretly excited he was coming over.

She fixed her white, sleeveless shirt again for probably the thirtieth time in the mirror. She would tuck it in and then pull it out. She couldn't decide if she wanted to look neat or slouchy.

She had on a pair of black, Nike shorts and black flip-flops. She dabbed some lip-gloss on her lips and put her silver cross necklace on. She had some passion fruit body spray from the local store in town. She liked the way it smelled although it wasn't very expensive or the most glamorous thing to wear. She lightly sprayed the insides of her wrists and rubbed them together.

When she was satisfied with the way she looked, she walked downstairs and found her mom slipping her leather pocket book over her shoulder.

"Oh, sweetie. I'm glad you finally came down. Don't you look good, today," her mom commented as she gave her daughter a once over inspection.

"Are you leaving?" Paige asked, panicking slightly. "Mom, you can't leave."

"Yes, I forgot to tell you I'm having a lunch/dinner date with Walter. It's for business, of course. I'll be home late, though," she said. "Don't wait up."

"Mom, Rocky is coming over here later today. I really needed you here."

"I thought you might like some time to talk things through. You don't need me hovering," she said. "You'll be fine."

"What if..what if I forgive him?" Paige asked, sounding much younger than she was. "What if I don't?"

"I know you'll do the right thing," she answered and patted her shoulder. Paige mumbled a goodbye and watched as her mom got in her car, pulled out of the driveway and disappeared down the road leaving her to face him alone.

Paige was frustrated. She wanted him to come over all ready so they could hash it out and put it behind them. She had no idea what they were even going to say. She was so nervous she paced the living room for the better part of the afternoon.

Finally, she heard a car door shut. She knew it was Rocky. She sat on the couch and waited for the doorbell to ring. She wanted to pretend her heart didn't jump up in her throat when the doorbell sounded, but it did. She went to open the door and stared at him for a minute before saying anything. His face was blank and his eyes were guarded.

"May I come in?" he finally asked her. She cleared her throat and nodded her head. She held the door open for him as he entered the foyer.

She noticed his hair was wet, so he had just taken a shower. He smelled like soap and some kind of amazing cologne. He had on a pair of khaki shorts, an Under Armor tank and tennis shoes. She could stare at him all day.

"You didn't text me. You look beat," she

commented, thinking a little small talk might help break the ice and keep her on the right track.

"Yeah, it was a rough practice and sorry, but I was afraid if I texted, you might not answer the door. The Coach really put it to Jazz and myself. I guess we deserved it, though. We did lose the game."

"I'm sorry you lost," Paige said. She really did hate they'd lost the game. He just nodded. There was a short, uncomfortable silence between them. Rocky wouldn't quit looking at her and she wanted to look anywhere but at him. Finally, Paige drew in a deep breath. "You want to go to the living room so we can sit down?"

"That'd be great," he said. He motioned for her to lead the way. Paige walked into the living room and sat down in one of the chairs closest to the door. She didn't want to sit on the coach. She was afraid he might try to sit beside her and being near him might cloud her thoughts.

The uncomfortable silence fell on them again. Paige was biting her lip when she looked up at him. He smiled for the first time since he'd arrived.

"This is a first," he said.

"What?"

"We've never had any trouble talking to one another before," he said.

"I guess, I just don't know what to say. I mean there's a lot I would like to say, but when I try, I just freeze up."

"Let me go first," he said. "I want to tell you again how sorry I am. Last year, I was a jerk." Paige almost cracked a smile, because that was exactly what she'd been thinking all day. "All I cared about was looking cool or getting a laugh out of my so called friends. You have to know I'm not like that anymore," he pleaded.

"I'll admit you're different than you were last year, but that doesn't make up for what you did."

"You're right."

"I want to know," Paige started.

"I'll tell you anything," he said.

"I want to know when you planned the prank, the whole story, beginning to end." He let out a sigh, but nodded.

"Okay, we saw the flyers you'd hung up all over school."

"Who's we?" she asked.

"Jazz, Roman and myself," he answered. He waited until she nodded before continuing. "I actually saw you hanging one up an afternoon after school. When you walked off, I went over and tore it down, wadded it up and threw it on the ground. I showed Jazz and told him someone should rain on your parade. I didn't mean it literally, but Jazz jumped on that. He told me I should do something. He said I would be the Master of Cool if I did something to ruin your prayer group. I went home that evening and all I could think about was how cool I would be. Then, I remembered the sprinklers. I knew exactly how to rain on your parade, literally. I came to school early that morning, snuck in the maintenance room and reset the timer for the sprinklers. Then, I texted all the football team, cheerleaders and anyone else I could think of. We were all standing in the school watching out the windows, waiting for the sprinklers to go off. You had more people there than I expected, but as soon as the water started flying, the people scattered. We were snapping pictures and laughing. They were patting me on the back and that's all that mattered to me then. So each time I heard about your prayer group, I did it, until one day you didn't have it anymore." He looked up at her and Paige had silent tears running down her face. "Paige, you have to know I'm not that guy anymore."

"Did you feel bad about it?"

"Of course, I feel bad about it. I would take it back if I could," he said.

"No, did you feel bad about it last year?"

He hesitated a few moments, but finally answered, "No."

"How could you? How could you do that to another person? Who were you?" Paige rattled off. "You don't understand what it was like. People made fun of me even more. They called me all kinds of names, but I didn't let it bother me. I continued on because I felt like God wanted me to. I felt like for the first time in my life, I actually mattered."

"Paige, you do matter," he interrupted. "You matter to a lot of people."

"It's so easy for you to say that, Mr. Popular Quarterback. The guy who matters to everyone at Valley High. You're the guy everyone wants to be friends with. The guy every girl wants to date. The guy teachers give homework free passes to so you can play football on Fridays without the worry of a lower GPA. You're the guy everyone loves. Do you know who I am? I'm the girl everyone either overlooks or people make fun of. I'm the girl you did that to. I'm the one people laughed at and I'm the one who felt like a complete failure for it."

"I'm so sorry, Paige. You have to know you matter, Paige. You're not a failure at all. I've never known anyone like you before."

"I know I matter to God. I matter to my Mom. I matter to Meghan and I have a few friends at church, but if I didn't come back to Valley High, no one would miss me besides Meghan. I'm no one."

"I would miss you because you are someone to me," he responded.

"Don't say things you don't mean," she warned.

"I'm not."

"When I started that group, I felt empowered for the first time in high school. People acted interested and I felt needed. I guess that sounds silly to someone like you."

"It doesn't sound silly. Everyone needs to feel that way," he said. "I wish I hadn't done it, but I can't take it back now. I can't make it go away. All I can do is beg you to forgive me and try to make it up to you somehow. I could tell you I was sorry until I was blue in the face, but the ball's in your court. You can forgive me or not, but there's one more thing you need to know. From the moment I saw you on the floor in front of our History class, I felt something for you." Paige looked up at him then with a guarded, confused expression. She wasn't sure where he was going with this. "At first, I thought I just wanted to protect you and make sure you didn't end up like my cousin, Avery. Then, I got to know you and found out how incredibly wonderful you truly are. You're so beautiful and caring." Paige inhaled deeply. No one had ever said that to her before and her heart skipped a beat. He was looking at her like she was the only thing that mattered to him.

"Rocky, please just stop. You don't have to say this stuff because you feel bad about what you did last year."

"I'm not just saying it because of the guilt I feel. I've wanted to tell you for a long time. You became such a big part of my life so quickly. I started to look forward to seeing you and talking to you in school. Before I even knew what was happening, I totally fell for you, Paige Jones." She just stared at him, without saying anything. When he couldn't take it anymore, he said, "This is the part where you say something."

"I wasn't expecting this," she admitted. He stood and walked over to her. She stood as well. He took her hand in his.

"I know. I'm surprised I'm even telling you now. Believe me, I'm not saying this to get you to forgive me, or anything like that. I just thought you needed to know exactly where I stand and exactly how I feel. More than anything in this world, I want you to forgive me. I want my friend back. I want us to be more than friends," he said. He stated at her until she wasn't able to take it anymore. She looked down and quickly pulled her hand away. She walked over to the window. She needed to put some space between them. This is what every girl in Valley High had always wanted to hear from Rocky West. Here he was in her living room pouring out his heart to her. She turned back to him.

"I forgive you, Rocky," she said. She smiled as she watched him visibly relax.

"Does this mean we're friends again?" he asked, sounding hopeful.

"I don't know," she said. He looked like she'd just hurt him, but she wanted to be truthful. "I need space and some time to figure this out."

"I can do space," he said. "I'm not giving up on you, Paige Jones. I'm fighting for our friendship and fighting for what could be the best thing that has ever happened to the two of us." She just stared at him again. She was completely taken back by the way he talked to her. She pinched herself on the arm to make sure she wasn't dreaming. Unfortunately, she pinched herself so hard; it was going to leave a mark.

"So, will you call me?" he asked.

"Yes, when and if I'm ready to talk, I'll call," she said.

"I'll be waiting on you. I won't text, call or come by, or at least not until I hear from you saying this is what you want. I want us, Paige. We belong together," he said. Then, he turned around and started toward the front door. She followed him.

"Thank you for coming here and telling me. I felt like I deserved to know," Paige said.
"Yes, you did. I'm glad you let me come. I finally got that off my chest along with a lot more. I hope I hear from you soon," he said. Paige only smiled and nodded. "I guess this is goodbye."

Paige didn't want to say goodbye, not like this. She wanted to tell him she would call him, but she held off. She just said bye and watched as he walked out to his car and backed out of her driveway. She needed to process her thoughts and her feelings. She closed the door and locked it. She walked straight up to her bedroom and threw herself down on her bed and prayed.

Heavenly Father, he just told me he cared about me. He told me he fell for me. That's what I've wanted to hear for so long and yet I can't do anything about it because he's not a Christian. Help me, Lord. Help me to deal with my feelings for him. Lord, please save his soul. Not because I want a boyfriend, but because he needs eternal life and he needs to realize that. Lord, please send him someone who can guide him. Thank you, Lord, for all your many blessings and allowing me the opportunity to talk to you. In your precious holy name, Amen.

Paige lay there a long time. She waited for her mom to get back home that evening before she got out of bed. She felt some better after she had prayed, but she was still conflicted in her heart. She just had to keep praying for God to work things out for his will.

CHAPTER TEN

Rocky drove through town just thinking about everything Paige had said. He'd told her he'd fell for her, but she couldn't tell him back. Maybe she didn't feel that way about him, but he had a feeling something else was holding her back. If only he knew what it was, maybe he could help her see past it. Maybe it was because of what he'd done last year, but she said she'd forgiven him. She knew he wasn't the same person.

He found himself driving and then parking at his usual spot on the side of the road by the graveyard. He headed up the now familiar path, straight to Avery's grave. He knelt down when he reached the tombstone and audibly sighed.

"Hey," he said, quietly. He'd give anything to hear her voice one more time. To be able to joke with her and to tease her about her ponytail she always insisted wearing. "I know I'm earlier than usual today. I just needed to talk to someone. You've always been the one I've talked to and confided in about everything. I finally got up the nerve to tell Paige I'd fallen for her. You remember me telling you about Paige, right? Well, she didn't tell me she was into me or anything like that. I know, shocker, right?" he said and smiled to himself. He could almost hear Avery's laughter and the ribbing she would give him about someone finally being able to resist his obvious charm and charisma. "I'm sure you're getting a big kick out of this."

"I need you, Avery. I need you here with me. Why did you do this? Why did you leave me and our family behind?" he asked as he felt the tiny bit of frustration toward her. He felt tears burning the back of his eyes, but he refused to let them come. No, he wouldn't break down. He was stronger than this. He felt guilty for speaking that way to her tombstone. "Look, you should have just come to me. I could have taken care of everything. I thought things were okay. I thought you were okay. I guess I was wrong," he said and shook his head. He needed to change the subject before he lost it.

"Anyhow, Paige is the girl for me. I've just got to keep showing her I care until I win her over," he said. "You know how it is when I put my mind to something," he said and chuckled to himself and wiped the one tear that dared to fall down his face away.

"Rocky?" he heard a female voice say from behind. He quickly stood up and swirled around. He was angry at the person behind him. They shouldn't have been listening to him and they needed to mind their own business.

"Monica, hey," he said, but his frustration was evident. He grimaced as he looked at the church youth group leader. He hoped she hadn't heard what he'd said. He stood there looking uncomfortable.

"I didn't mean to interrupt you. You just looked like you might need a friend," she said. For some reason, what she said made him all the more furious. Who was she to tell him what he needed? He'd wanted to lash out at someone over Avery's death since it happened.

"Who do you think you are to tell me what I need? You don't know me. All you want to do is shove your religious point of view down my throat. Yeah, my cousin killed herself. She cut her wrist and let herself bleed all over everything," he shouted. "God could have stopped her, but he didn't. An innocent young girl was robbed of her life because of narrow minded people."

"Rocky, I'm so sorry. I didn't mean to intrude. I didn't mean to make you feel bad or like I was overstepping."

"Of course, you did. That's what all you people do. You won't listen to me. You let me down. You..you..you didn't come to me when you needed me. You took the coward's way out. You left us. You left us," he screamed. What Rocky didn't realize was that he'd turned his anger from Monica and God to Avery. He felt a sob coming up out of his chest and he wasn't able to contain it anymore. He hit the ground beside her grave and cried. It was the first time he'd cried since he found her body. It was the first time he'd showed any kind of outward emotion since her funeral. He'd just bottled up everything inside and he couldn't handle it anymore. He knelt there for a long time and finally felt Monica kneel down next to him. He wouldn't look at her. He wouldn't acknowledge her. Finally, she placed her hand on his shoulder. It was a simple gesture. He hadn't allowed anyone to comfort him. Not his parents and certainly not Avery's parents. He'd gone out of his way to comfort everyone else. Now, this woman who barely knew him offered him a hand and he felt comforted. He quickly dashed his tears away with the back of his hand and looked up at her.

"I'm sorry. I don't know what came over me. I don't do that. I don't lash out at people like that unexpectedly," he apologized. She smiled at him.

"It sounded like you needed to get some of that out," she answered. He began walking back to his car and she followed. She waited until he said something.

"It's so wrong of me to be angry with her," he said.

"I think anger is a typical emotion we have when dealing with the death of a loved one."

"You know; she was more like my sister. We were both an only child and our families were close. When I walked in and found her dead, it was like my world stopped. She took her own life. She could have come to me. I would have taken care of anyone bothering her. Anyone. She chose not to tell me, though. She chose to leave me, leave all of us. I don't understand that. I also don't understand why God didn't stop her."

"Maybe, you don't understand because you haven't been in her shoes. None of us know what was going on in her head when she did that. I'm sure she wouldn't want you to be angry with yourself. It's not our place to question God, even when we don't understand."

"What?"

"Maybe you're angry with her and God or just maybe you're angry with yourself for not being able to help her."

"Yeah, I think you're right," he said, quietly. There

was a bench at the gate of the cemetery and she asked him if he would like to sit down and talk. He nodded and they both moved to sit down on the iron bench. "I don't know how to move on. I've never lost anyone before and all I see every day is her lifeless body and the blood and I can't shake it. I can't let it go. I need to. I need some kind of peace. Don't get me wrong. I don't want to forget her, but I can't keep bottling all of this emotion inside. I think that's one reason why I was so drawn to Paige at first. I saw someone bullying her and I vowed I wouldn't watch another person feel like the only way out was to take their own life."

"Things seemed to have developed into a little more than that with Paige now," Monica commented.

"For me, but I'm not so sure about her," he said.

"God has a way of working things out," she replied.

"Do you truly believe that? When I think about God, all I feel is…lost."

"Rocky, have you ever asked the Lord to live in your heart?" He shook his head no. "Do you believe in God, Rocky?"

"Of course, I do."

"Do you believe Jesus Christ died on the cross for your sins?"

"I've heard that in church."

"It has to be more than hearing. You either believe or you don't," Monica said to him pointedly. "Jesus would have died if you had been the only one he died for. That's how much he loves you."

"Yes, I believe," Rocky said and in that moment, he truly did.

"Do you believe Jesus rose from the dead?" she asked. He nodded.

"Acts 16:31 says, Believe on the Lord Jesus Christ, and thou shalt be saved, and thy house. Romans 10: 9-10 says, That if thou shalt confess with thy mouth the Lord Jesus, and believe in thine heart that God hath raised him from the dead, thou shalt be saved. For with the heart man believeth unto righteousness, and with the mouth confession is made unto salvation. Rocky, do you want the blessed assurance and peace God will give you when you ask him to live in your heart?" she asked. Rocky stared at her for a few minutes and then everything became so clear. This was what his life was missing. This is what he wanted all along.

"Yes, yes. This is what I need. What do I do?" he asked her. They were tears in her eyes as she looked at him now.

"You need to confess you are a sinner and ask God's forgiveness for that. Believe on the Lord and ask him to come into your heart and be the Lord of your life." Rocky wasn't sure if it was that easy. He had to make the decision to admit he was a sinner. Rocky already knew that. He'd done a lot of things wrong. He had to believe in Jesus. He already did that. He had to ask God to forgive him and ask him to live in his heart.

Rocky put his hands over his face and prayed a simple prayer. "Jesus, this is Rocky. I'm sorry for everything. I've partied too much and did many things I'm ashamed of. I've lived a life I'm not proud of. I'm a sinner, God. Please forgive me for it all. I believe you died for me and rose again and I'm asking you God to live in my heart. I need peace only you can give. I need that comfort from you and I need assurance in this life that I'm going to be okay. Amen." When Rocky looked up, he was crying again and Monica was too.

"Rocky, I think that's the best prayer I've ever heard," she said and didn't even try to hide the fact she was crying. She hugged him and he hugged her back. "How do you feel?"

Rocky looked at her, hesitating for a moment so he could try to figure out the words he needed to say. "I feel like a new man."

"Praise the Lord. You can't begin to understand how happy and proud I am of you and how happy Jesus is that you've finally accepted him as your Savior."

"Thank you," Rocky said. He wasn't sure what else to say to Monica. He was so grateful to her for being there when he felt so low and talking to him. "I'm glad you were here."

"Me too," she said. "I bet Paige will be delighted to hear this. Are you going to call her or just go straight over there?"

"I'm giving Paige some space right now. I don't want to bombard her or make her think this is my way of getting back on her good side."

"Well, I can understand, but I know when she does find out, she'll be thrilled." Monica saw Rocky looking back up toward Avery's grave. "Do you need some time alone?"

"Yeah, I think I might go back up there a few minutes. Thanks, Monica."

"I'll see you in the morning," she said.

"I'll be there," he responded.

"Oh and Rocky?" Monica called.

"Yeah?" he answered.

"Don't give up on Paige," she said.

"Trust me, I don't intend to," he answered and waved.

He walked back up the hill and knelt down once more by her grave. "I'm sorry, Avery. I shouldn't have lashed out at your memory. I don't know what you were going through and I wish I had. I would have tried to help. I just accepted the Lord into my heart. I got saved, Avery. If you were here, you'd be happy for me. I wish you were here. I love you, girl." Rocky felt new tears running down his face, but for the first time, he didn't push them away. Rocky stood back up and walked down the hill toward his car, feeling lighter than he'd felt in months. Things still might not be perfect in his life. His cousin's death was still very fresh to him. Paige wasn't going to cut him any slack, but he had a God who would help him get through everything. That thought alone made him feel better. He started up his car and headed home wishing he could call Paige and tell her his good news.

Paige was sitting on her bed reading a book when her phone rang that evening. She hoped it wasn't Rocky, but if it were she wouldn't answer it. Instead, she looked and saw it was Monica. She quickly answered delighted her youth leader was calling her.

"Hey, Monica," Paige said.

"Hey, Paige. How are you?"

"I'm okay," she answered, not wanting to get into anything with Monica about Rocky.

"Did you have a good birthday?" she asked.

"Well, it could have been better, but it was fine."

"I have something to tell you. I thought you might like to know and I'm assuming you don't know already."

"What is it?" Paige said. Her interest perked up. She thought maybe Monica had a new song for the youth group or something for them to learn.

"I got to witness someone getting saved this evening. I thought maybe they would have called you earlier, so I wanted to wait just in case."

"No. No one's called me. That's great news, though. Who was it?"

"Rocky," Monica said. She heard Paige's sharp intake of breath. She wasn't able to say anything for several minutes. "Paige, you still with me?"

"Yes," she finally got out. "I just don't know what to say. When? I mean, where? How? My Rocky? I mean, he's not mine. I just…. I just…."

"Calm down. I'll tell you everything," Monica said and laughed at Paige's enthusiastic response. "I was at the cemetery this afternoon placing flowers on my grandmother's grave. I looked up and saw Rocky knelt down beside his cousin's grave. He looked so alone, liked he'd lost his best friend. I felt like the Lord was leading me to go to him. I called his name and he turned around. He wasn't happy to see me. He actually lashed out at me. He started yelling but instead of being angry with me, he started yelling at Avery."

"Avery? His cousin?" Paige asked, confused. "I'm not following."

"Well, apparently he's going through the anger part of his grief. He'd been holding in so much. He was angry because she didn't confide in him. He was angry with himself for not being there for her. He was angry with her for killing herself and leaving her family behind."

"Oh my. I knew he was still hurting over her death,

but I had no idea all that was going on inside of him. He hides it well," Paige responded.

"He knelt down at her grave and he cried. He apologized and ended up walking down to the gate with me and we started talking. He didn't know what to do or how he could move forward. I started telling him about Jesus and accepting him as his Savior. He was very receptive and prayed the most earnest sinner's prayer. When I left him, he was heading back up to Avery's grave again. He said he would be at church tomorrow, so maybe he was just going to wait and tell you there."

"I asked him for some space," Paige said.

"Yes, he told me that," Monica said.

"What else did he say about me?" Paige asked.

"Not a lot, but I know he's crazy about you. You can tell that just by the way he talks," she said.

"I don't know," Paige said.

"Just pray about it. God will work things out the way he wants them to be. Have faith, sweetie."

"Thanks, Monica. I really appreciate you calling me and telling me."

"Sure thing. See you in the morning."

"See ya," Paige said and then hung up her phone. She was full of excited energy now. Rocky had gotten saved. She was thrilled. She wanted to call him. Was an afternoon of space enough? No, she had to talk to him in person. She was just talk to him after church tomorrow.

She slid in the bed that night knowing sleep wouldn't come for a long time. Her mom had just gotten home and claimed exhaustion. She'd headed straight to bed, so Paige had decided to turn in. She lay in bed thinking about everything. She was praying for him while he got saved. What a blessing.

Dear Heavenly Father, I don't have enough words to express how thankful I am for you saving Rocky's soul today. I was praying, feeling hopeless that things could ever work out for him and me because he wasn't saved. I asked you to send someone to guide him and you sent Monica. Thank you so much for that, for saving his soul and for answering prayers. I love you, Lord. Amen.

CHAPTER ELEVEN

Paige got up early on Sunday morning, showered and started getting ready for church. She was so excited to see Rocky and congratulate him on getting saved. She picked out a purple dress that flared just a little in the hips and came down past her knees and white sandals to match. She put her hair back in a braid and applied a small amount of makeup. She didn't want to overdo, but she wanted to look good.

She went down to the kitchen and her mom was sitting at the table looking grumpy and barely awake. Paige smiled while she grabbed a water bottle from the fridge and snatched an apple out of the bowl of fruit on the table. She walked over to her mom.

"You seem chipper this morning," Ellen said, eyeing her daughter. Paige could have laughed at her mom. Her mom wasn't a morning person and she didn't even like to talk that much before she'd had about three cups of coffee.

"Good morning to you. I'm headed to church early," she said with obvious enthusiasm. Ellen nodded blankly and went back to reading a trashy novel, which Paige hated. "Would you like to come with me? I can wait."

"No, no. You go on. I'll just stay at home and enjoy my day off," Ellen said. She picked up her novel and walked to the back deck with her coffee in her hand. Paige felt a little disheartened at her mom's lack of concern for her soul, but she wouldn't let that ruin her excitement over Rocky.

She went and started her car. She texted Meghan to tell her she was getting there early and for her to hurry up before she pulled out of her driveway. She needed Meghan's confidence to help her before Rocky got there.

When Paige pulled in the parking lot at church, Meghan was already at church looking like her gorgeous self. Paige wondered how Meghan always looked so good. She had long, gorgeous blond hair, Caribbean Sea blue eyes, and a figure anyone would die for. Meghan was wearing a skirt with stripes and a pale blue shirt that matched. Only someone like Meghan could pull off that outfit and look like a million bucks.

"How did you get here so quick?" Paige asked.

"Girl, I'm always on the ball. When I got your text, I knew you needed me so I just left early, too. So, what's up?" Meghan asked.

"Rocky got saved yesterday," Paige said. She wanted to jump up and down to show her excitement. "Can you believe that?"

"Oh my gosh. That's awesome! When? Were you with him?"

"No, actually it was right after he left my house. Monica ran into him at the cemetery."

"Creepy," Meghan said. Paige rolled her eyes at her friend's antics but continued.

"Anyhow, they got to talking and Monica led him to the Lord. I can't wait to see him."

"I bet you were totally psyched when he told you," Meghan commented.

"Well, actually Monica called and told me." Paige let a little of her doubt shine through right then. She had actually hoped he would call her last night, if only to share his good news with her.

"What? He didn't call you?" Meghan asked.

"No. I told him I needed space, so he didn't call."
"Why didn't you call him? Seriously, this is a big deal, Paige."

"I know that, but what I have to say, I wanted to say to him in person," Paige defended herself.

"Sometimes, you're so weird."

"That's not weird, Meghan." Just then, they heard the chiming of the church bells telling them it was time to start. "He's not here yet."

"Isn't his parents always late?" Meghan asked.

"Yes, that's true."

"Just because he gave his heart to the Lord, doesn't mean his parents will be punctual." Meghan said that with such a stern look, it made Paige laugh. "Come on. Let's get inside before the service starts. You can talk to him just as soon as church is over."

"Yeah, you're right."

The girls walked in and sat down in their usual spot with Kaylee and Abby sitting next to them. Paige kept glancing back at the door until he came walking through with his parents. He looked so gorgeous. He had on a black polo shirt and a pair of jeans. He caught her looking at him and he smiled at her before he quickly looked away. Paige felt at ease. He was there and she was going to talk to him right after church. Everything would be right in the world.

When church was over, Paige quickly jumped up and tried to head outside. Kaylee stopped her and asked her a question about a problem she was having. Paige couldn't leave without talking to her, so she sat her down on the bench as Kaylee poured her heart out to Paige. They'd probably been sitting there fifteen minutes before Kaylee hugged her and thanked her for listening. Paige knew without a doubt he was gone. She quickly hurried outside though on the off chance he'd waited. Unfortunately, all she saw was Kaylee getting into her parents' car and Meghan waiting for her.

"What happened to you?" Meghan asked.

"Kaylee needed someone to talk to," Paige explained. "Did you see him?"

"Yes, but I really didn't get to talk to him. He was talking to the Pastor and then Monica. The last I saw of him, he was getting into his parents' car and they drove away. I'm thinking now is the time for you to call him. Better yet, go to his house and surprise him."

"I don't think I can do that," she said.

"Of course you can. You have to. You're meant to be with him, Paige. Why can't you see it? You've been fighting this since the beginning of the year," Monica said. She was clearly getting frustrated with Paige.

"You know why I held back," Paige said, accusingly.

"Yes, but now you have to make the next move. He isn't going to continue to pursue you when you plainly told him to back off. If you want to be with this boy, then do something about it."

"Okay then, I will, first thing in the morning."

"Well, it better be good," Meghan said. "Why don't you come over to the house? Mom is cooking her famous spaghetti and we'll talk about what you have planned."

"Okay, I'll just text my mom." Paige got into her car and followed Meghan. She already knew exactly what she was going to do when she saw him. It wasn't extravagant but coming from her, it would be huge.

Rocky had noticed Paige looking at him multiple times during the church service. He tried telling himself not to expect too much from her. She obviously still needed space or she would have come outside after church. He was trying not to let anyone see, but he was scanning the crowd for her.

He was driving to school on Monday morning and he was looking forward to at least seeing her. They still had History together. Maybe they could talk then. Maybe she would be in a forgiving mood when he told her what happened on Saturday.

He pulled into his usual parking space. The football team was there as usual. Most of the cheerleaders were there, too, including Veronica who was hanging on Jazz like her life depended on it. Rocky stepped out of the car after grabbing his gym bag. He threw it over his shoulder and faced his crowd. He wasn't sure how to act around them. He knew he wasn't going to be able to hang with them and live a Christian life. He didn't really know what to do, or how to act.

"Rockman," several of his teammates screamed. He nervously laughed at his nickname, bumped a few fists and nodded his head at everyone else including Jazz who was standing in the background. That was when he saw her coming through the crowd. She looked ready for battle.

"What does she think she's doing?" he heard Veronica sneer. "She doesn't belong here. Who does she think she is?"

Paige was walking up to him without even acknowledging what she'd just heard. She looked unbelievable. Her hair was long and straight, just the way he liked it. She had on a pair of khaki shorts and a tie-dye shirt that was tucked in. She was so small. She was wearing flip-flops and her sunglasses were perched on top of her head. She looked like a woman on a mission.

"Paige, what are you?" Rocky started to ask, but was cut short when she threw herself in his arms. He wasn't expecting the hug and he had to catch himself. He let his gym bag fall to the ground as he hugged her back. He knew everyone was watching them, but he didn't care. He breathed in her scent. She smelled like honeysuckle and shampoo. He smiled. That was her scent.

"I'm so proud of you," she mumbled while she was still hugging him. Realization dawned on him. She knew he'd given his heart to the Lord.

"Who told you?" he asked.

"Monica," she explained. "Don't be mad at her. She wanted to give me some good news."

"I'm not mad," he said as he pulled her back just enough to see her face. He searched her eyes, wanting with all his heart for her to tell him things were okay with them.

"No more space," she said, quietly staring back at him.

"What?" he asked. He couldn't believe what she was saying to him.

"I don't want any space from you."

"So, does that mean we're okay?" he asked.

"Yes," she whispered. "Better than okay."

"Okay, I've got to know, does this mean we're together? Does this mean you're my girl?"

"Are you asking me to be your girl?" she said, and smiled at him. It was hard not to notice they had an audience, but Paige didn't care. She was the happiest girl right then.

"Yes, I'm most definitely asking you," he said and flashed her a grin. She smiled again at him.

"Then, yes, I'm your girl," she said. He pulled her back into a tight hug. He wanted to kiss her, but he also didn't want to scare her off. He felt like someone had just given him a million dollars, but he knew a mere million wouldn't compare to the treasure he held right then. He didn't think he'd ever been happier. He was saved and Paige was his girlfriend. What more could a guy ask for?

"Well, isn't that just the sweetest thing?" he heard Veronica say in a sarcastic voice. "What do you think girls? Swoon worthy?"

"Oh, totally, V. I think I shed a tear," Molly said, and pretended to flick a tear away. They both laughed. Some of the other cheerleaders laughed, but others waited to see how Rocky would handle this.
Rocky loosened his hold on Paige and he slid his hand in hers. He picked his gym bag up off the ground and walked toward V.

"I guess this means you'll congratulate us and be happy." He was looking at her and then at Jazz. Rocky wanted to be ready for anything. He wasn't sure what Jazz would do, but apparently he was letting V fight her own battles that day. He stayed in the back of the crowd, just watching everything.

"Of course, Rocky. I've only wanted the best for you

and now you have it," she said, looking Paige up and down. Then, she rolled her eyes. Molly walked up beside her to show Rocky who's side she was on. "I can't argue with that," Rocky said. He gave Paige's hand a gentle squeeze. "I'm glad to see you can leave the past in the past and move on. Right, V?"

"Anything for you, Rockman," she threw at him like it was a slur more than a nickname. He decided it was time to walk off from his crew and head in to school.

"Oh, Paige?" Veronica said, faking sweetness. "Don't ever let it be said I didn't warn you. You know, girl code and all? When he gets tired of you, and he will, he'll drop you so fast it will make your head spin. Just me being your friend," she said and laughed again.

"Come on. I'm not listening to her anymore," he said. He pulled Paige along and they walked in the school and literally ran straight into Meghan.

"So, are you two official yet?" Meghan asked. Paige nodded her head and held up her hand, which still had his securely intertwined with hers. Meghan then looked to Rocky and he smiled and nodded, too.

"Shew, it's about time," she said. They all laughed at that.

"Well, since I finally have my guy, maybe I should start concentrating on my best friend and her love life. She needs a guy, too."

"Oh no, thank you," Meghan said.

"I know plenty of guys," Rocky started, but Paige and Meghan both cut him off with a loud no. Rocky busted out laughing. "Come on. Not all of us are like Jazz."

"I'll find my own guy, thank you very much," Meghan said. "Well, I'm off to class. Text me later."

Paige nodded and then turned back to Rocky.

"What now?" she asked.

"Well, I think we should start our first official day being a couple with me walking you to your class," he said and winked.

"How kind of you since it's your class, too," she said and giggled. He smiled back at her and brought her hand up to his lips and softly kissed it. She blushed again.

"I could totally get used to the whole blushing thing. It's adorable," he said.

The rest of the week Paige and Rocky spent as much time as possible together. She stayed and watched practice every day. He picked her up for school and took her home every day. On Friday night, she, Meghan and their friends were back at the football game cheering him on. Rocky had never been happier.

They won their game that night. He told Paige she was his good luck charm, but she argued with him. She said he didn't need luck. He had God on his side. He couldn't argue with that.

When he dropped her off on Friday, he told her to be ready the next evening at six.

"What for?" she asked.

"It's a surprise," he commented, "and you won't get me to tell. I can keep a secret, little miss."

"Fine, but do I need to dress up or wear jeans. You have to give me a clue."

"Okay, dress up," he said.

"Hmm....this sounds interesting."

Rocky was staring at her. She was the most beautiful creature on this planet. He couldn't look away. "Would I scare you if I kissed you right now?"

"No," she said, quietly.

"May I kiss you, Paige Jones?"

She smiled and said, "Yes, you may Rocky West."
He leaned over to her and touched her lips with his own.
He easily slid his hands around her waist as she slid her
arms around his neck. When he pulled away, she smiled
again and he caressed her cheek. Her first kiss was just
as she imagined it would be. It was breathtaking and
overwhelming. It was also wonderful.

"I've fallen hard for you," Rocky said.

"Me too," Paige answered. He quickly kissed her
again and then promised to see her at six the next
evening. She went in the house walking in a dream like
state all the way up to her room.
The last thing she remembers before drifting off into a
welcome sleep was his simple text.

Night beautiful.

CHAPTER TWELVE

Rocky showed up at Paige's house right on time at six. He walked up to her front door and knocked with a bouquet of flowers in his hand. Her mom opened the door and looked at him without smiling or anything like that.

"I assume you're Rocky," Ellen said. She hadn't asked him to come in yet. She just stood there staring him down. Rocky nervously cleared his throat before answering.

"Yes, ma'am," he said. "These are for you." Ellen took the flowers, but still looked skeptical without even glancing at the flowers in his hand.

"And just where are you taking my daughter tonight?" she asked.

"Well, it's a surprise, but I'm taking her down to my parent's pond. I've set up a table and we're having supper, just the two of us. I hope she likes it. I thought that would suit her better than going out to some fancy restaurant."

"Are you saying my daughter isn't good enough for some fancy restaurant?"

"No, ma'am," Rocky stuttered. "It's just that she

seems like the kind of girl who would appreciate sitting by a pond, eating our supper and just watching the scenery. It's very peaceful there."

"Mom? Is that Rocky?" Paige called when she came downstairs.

"Yes, dear," Ellen shouted, still never taking her eyes off of the boy standing on the doorstep.

"Well, let him in," Paige answered.

"I'm thinking about it," Ellen shouted back. Paige walked up behind her mom and poked her head around. She smiled at Rocky and wanted to laugh when he looked relieved to see her.

"Don't worry about her. She's just giving you a hard time. She's not serious," Paige said. Rocky chanced a glance at Ellen and she was smiling with a teasing glint in her eye. "Mom, you had him scared to death."

"Oh, I'll have to write this one down," she said as she patted him on the back. "I couldn't resist and you fell for it so easily. By the way, these flowers are beautiful."

"Yes, ma'am I did fall for it, but I have to hand it to you. You should be an actress. You were so believable. Oh and nothing but the best for you." He winked at her.

"Please don't tell her that. She'll only get the big head," Paige laughed.

"Sweetie, can I help the boy sees raw talent and knows what kind of flowers to buy?" Ellen teased, good naturedly. Rocky and Paige both laughed at her. "Okay, off with both of you. Rocky, I trust you will take care of my girl."

"Yes, ma'am. I intend to."

"Call me Ellen," she said with a smile.

"Yes, ma'am, I mean Ellen, ma'am," he said and Paige and Ellen both laughed at him. He just rolled his eyes and ushered her on out the door. Paige had borrowed some of Meghan's clothes for the evening, but she felt like her skirt was too short and her blouse was too clingy.

"You look great," Rocky said. He seemed to notice she was uncomfortable with what she was wearing. He opened the car door for her and she slid into the passenger seat. He walked around the car, got in and started the car.

"Thank you for saying I look great, even though I don't feel like it myself. This outfit is Meghan's and it's really not me."

"I think you look beautiful no matter what you're wearing," he said. Paige smiled at him.

"Flattery will get you everywhere, sir," she said, playfully.

"Really?" he asked. She blushed and laced her hand through his as he drove with the other one.

When they got to Rocky's house and got out of the car, Paige looked confused. "I thought we were going out," she said.

"I have something special set up for you," he said. Paige smiled as he slid his hand in hers.

They walked around Rocky's house and continued past the pool, through the backyard, toward the woods. Paige was really starting to wonder what they were doing when they started walking along a dirt path.

"I'm really not dressed for hiking," Paige mumbled. Rocky only laughed and tugged at her hand, pulling her along. They continued until they came to an opening. Paige gasped when she saw the most beautiful sight she'd ever seen. There was a beautiful pond with a small island in the center. A wooden bridge went from the outer banks of the pond to the island and a gazebo was in the center of the island.

"It's beautiful," Paige sighed.

"You think?" Rocky asked.

"Yes, it's wonderful," Paige said.

"Come on," he said motioning for her to go to the bridge. She walked over the bridge, still looking at all their surroundings. The pond was set in the center of deep woods. It was peaceful and beautiful. Paige thought she would be content to stay here the rest of her life.

When they reached the island, he pulled her forward and she saw a table set up in the gazebo. There was a candle in the center. The gazebo had twinkle lights strung all over it.

"You did this for me?" Paige asked.

"Yeah," he said.

"I bet you do this for all your girls," Paige said, teasing him.

"Nope, you're the first one I've brought here," he said.

"Oh," she said. She didn't know what to say to that. He was so thoughtful.

"I wanted to do something for you to let you know just how important you are to me," he said.

"You may get tired of me after a while," Paige mumbled, showing a small bit of insecurity.

"Not a chance," he said. Paige looked up at him and smiled. He looked into her eyes and slowly lowered his mouth to hers for a quick kiss. Then, he turned around and pulled her chair out for her. She sat down wondering what kind of food he would have for them. "Okay, so I know you are basically a healthy eater. I'm not really a cook, so I went to Gilotti's and bought one of their famous salads you seem to like.

"Oh, that's sounds delicious," she said, smiling up at him.

He sat down across from her and asked her to pray before they ate. She smiled and said the blessing. Then, they dug in to the salad, both content to be with each other.

"This place is really beautiful. This should be our spot," she said.

"Well, it does help that my parents own it," Rocky said and winked at her. She laughed.

"Yeah, I guess it does." When they finished eating, they talked. Paige was so comfortable with him. They talked for hours about everything. School. Football. Church.

"Oh, we have to go before it gets dark," Rocky said, checking his phone for the time.

"Why?"

"There's someone I want you to meet," he said.

"Oh, okay."

Rocky and Paige quickly picked up the stuff from the table and slid it into the picnic basket he'd brought. Then, he took her hand in his and walked back across the bridge, through the woods and to his car.

They quickly drove to the cemetery and Paige knew Rocky came here often. His cousin was buried here.

They got out of the car and she slid her hand in his once again. They silently walked up the path to a tombstone. Paige knew Rocky had taken her death very hard.

"Hey, Avery," Rocky said, then turned to look at Paige. "I know it's crazy to talk to her grave like that, but it helps me cope a little."

"I don't think it's crazy. I think it makes perfect sense."

"Really?"

"Yeah," she said.

"I wanted you to meet her or at least come here with me and let me tell you about her."

"I'd love to hear about her," Paige answered him. She squeezed his hand, hoping to give him a little support.

"We were cousins, but we grew up more like brother and sister. She was my best friend. We spent lots of time together. Our families had always been close. We spent every holiday together. We went on vacations together. The only thing we didn't do was go to school together. She went to the high school across town. The private one. I know my aunt and uncle thought they were doing the right thing by not sending her to public school, but if she'd went to school with me, I could have watched out for her. I would have protected her from bullies and things like that. You know, the funny thing is, I used to be that kind of person. A bully. Someone who made fun of people and put other people down. I didn't care who I hurt. It wasn't until I found Avery and realized why she did what she did, that I started to think about what I was doing. I wanted to change. Then, I saw you on the floor in front of our history class. I lost it. All I could see was Avery."

"That must have been hard for you," Paige said.

"I mean, I knew you weren't her, but Jazz and Veronica treating you like that just made my blood boil. No one has the right to treat someone else that way."

"But I'm not Avery," Paige said. She wasn't really

sure what to think about where his conversation was going. Was that the draw he felt toward her? Was it more of a friend or sister feeling?

"No, you're not. Once I got in the classroom and asked you if you were okay, I finally saw you. I started watching for you at school. I noticed someone who'd been under my nose all these years and I'd never seen before. I wanted to protect you. At first, I told myself that was all it was. I wasn't interested, but the more I got to know you, the more interested I was in getting to know you more. I saw a beautiful girl full of compassion and love. I knew I wanted her in my life." He leaned up and kissed her cheek. She smiled back.

"Well, I guess you're lucky that I'm your girlfriend," she said, teasing him. "Tell me more about Avery."

"I found her. She was supposed to meet me that evening and she didn't show up. I went to check on her and found her. There was a lot of blood," he said and stopped a moment. His pain was evident and Paige hurt for him. "I'm not sure I'll ever get over it. Not really. Later, they found a note from her. Some girls were bullying her in school. They constantly made fun of her. They called her names, they hid her clothes one day when she was in gym and then snapped pictures of her. They posted them all over school. The principal told her parents they couldn't prove who did it. They stalked he on Facebook and tormented her with messages. They slashed her tires and even put a boy up to ask her out, just to dump her in front of the whole school. They did everything they could to get her to break. Why? Why do people treat others like that?"

"I wish I knew. I think sometimes it's because they lack self-confidence or maybe they aren't satisfied with their self so they put someone else down. They think if everyone is looking at another person, they won't notice their own mistakes and shortcomings."

"Wow, that makes a lot of sense."

"It's not right at all. I can't believe they did all of that to her."

"They tagged her locker. One day, they broke in her locker and dumped all her stuff out in the hall."

"Did she tell you this was going on?"

"No. She never mentioned a word about it. She knew I would come over there and put some people in their place."

"I wish she would have," Paige said.

"You don't know how many times I wished that very thing. She would have loved you. She would have said you were good for me."

"I wish I could have met her."

"She left a note telling us she couldn't take it anymore. She said she was tired of fighting."

"What happened to the kids who were doing that to her?"

"A couple of them were sent to juvenile detention. Some are still there, but there wasn't enough evidence to convict everyone."

"Do you know who they are?"

"Yeah, but they steer clear of me," he said.

"I'm so sorry, Rocky. Really, I am," Paige said, laying her head on his shoulder.

"So, I come here to talk to her. It makes me feel closer to her somehow and I wanted to share that with you," he said.

"I'm so glad you did," she said.

The sun had set now and it was getting dark. He

tugged her along back down to his car and they rode around. Paige was glad when he started talking about other things and some of the pain left his face. Her heart broke thinking of what Rocky and his family had been through. She wasn't sure exactly how she would have handled it. Finally, it was time for her to go home. Her curfew was almost up. He pulled into her driveway. Paige didn't want the night to end and wasn't in a hurry to get out of the car.

"Thank you for tonight," she said.

"You're welcome. Sorry I got all serious on you about Avery," he said.

"No, I'm glad you told me," she said.

"So, church tomorrow?"

"Yeah."

"Want a ride?"

"Definitely," she answered. There'd been another question she was hoping he would ask tonight, but he hadn't mentioned anything. He got out of the car and came around to open her door. She smiled at him as they walked to her door.

"So," she said.

"So," he answered.

"Next weekend is homecoming," Paige said.

"Yeah, I think we'll win, though. We've been working really hard."

"Of course you will and then there's the dance," she said. She was praying he would ask her to it.

"Yeah, most people go."

"Are you?" she asked.

"Well, that depends," he answered.

"On what?" she asked.

"If you'll go with me or not," he said. "Paige Jones,

will you be my date to homecoming?"

"Yes," she said and smiled. He chuckled and then leaned in to kiss her. She kissed him back as she slid her arms around his neck. When he broke the kiss, she couldn't stop smiling. He kissed the end of her nose.

"I'll see you in the morning," he said and walked back to his car. Paige stood on the porch and watched as he backed out of the driveway and left. She couldn't remember the last time she'd been this happy.

Trish Shaver

CHAPTER THIRTEEN

Meghan insisted she take Paige dress shopping Monday right after school. Paige wanted to wait for Rocky to finish up with football practice, but Meghan demanded to leave.

"Fine, fine," Paige teased. "You don't have to be so pushy." Paige sent Rocky a quick text telling him she was dress shopping with Meghan and she would talk to him later.

"Look, you're dating the quarterback of the football team. You need to have the most amazing dress. You need to turn heads."

"I'm not sure, Meghan. I mean, I don't want to stand out," Paige said, sounding very unsure of herself.

"Oh please, for one night, you need to stand out," Meghan said. She pulled her car into the parking lot of the dress shop on the corner of Main St. and Grayson. She almost dragged Paige out of the car and into the shop. Paige was laughing at Meghan's enthusiasm as they walked through the shop.

Meghan was gazing at each dress as if it was the best thing she'd ever seen. She would hold them up to Paige and smile or frown.

"So, who are you going to homecoming with?" Paige asked, feeling a little overwhelmed at all the attention she was getting. She wanted to think about something else for a moment.

"Why?" Meghan responded back, trying to sound as nonchalant as possible.

"Meghan, do you have a date?"

"Maybe," she answered, with a teasing glint in her eye. She pulled out a red dress covered with sequins and held it up for Paige's inspection. Paige gave her a skeptical look and Meghan hung the dress back up.

"Who? Tell me," Paige insisted. "I can't believe you haven't already told me. I mean, we're BFFs. What's up with that?"

"Look, it's no big deal," Meghan said, shrugging her shoulders. "I just didn't want you to get the wrong idea."

"Tell me now," Paige insisted, tapping her foot while Meghan pulled down a lime green dress and held it up. When Paige snarled her nose, Meghan put it back.

"Jake asked me," Meghan answered and shrugged her shoulders like it was no big deal.

"Oh my gosh, we can double." Paige squealed with delight. She was almost jumping up and down.

"Oh no, honey. This is your night. He just asked to be nice," Meghan said.

"Do you like him?"

"Eh, he's okay," Meghan said. Then, she turned her attention to the dresses. Paige wanted to talk more about her going to the dance with Jake, but she wouldn't hear it.

"No spark?" Paige asked.

"Just because you and Rocky have amazing chemistry, doesn't mean everyone will. Jake and I are friends and that's it."

Meghan turned around to the next rack of clothes and pulled out a gorgeous, white, silk dress. It was sleeveless with ties to go around the neck. It was fitted in the waist and then flared out slightly, coming just above the knee. The dress was soft and flowing. Meghan turned to Paige and held it up.

"This is it. This is the perfect dress," Meghan said.

"Oh my gosh. It's gorgeous," Paige said. She took the dress from Meghan and held it up to herself. It was just her size. She turned toward the mirror and looked at it with a smile.

"Try it on," Meghan said, enthusiastically. "Hurry." Paige took the dress from her friend and walked to the dressing room. An attendant was waiting to let her in one of the rooms. She quickly undressed and slid the dress on. It was perfect. She opened the door and went to look in the mirror. She wondered what Rocky would think of it as she twirled in front of the mirror. Then, she heard a shrill voice behind her.

"Wow, isn't that a pretty sight," hissed Veronica. Paige turned to look at her. Veronica was wearing the red, sequined dress Meghan had picked up earlier. It was skin tight and fit Veronica's slender frame perfect. "I guess you're Snow White. Too bad I don't have a poisonous apple."

"Seriously? That's the best you can do?" Paige asked, turning back around and looking in the mirror at her reflection. She felt plain compared to Veronica's glamorous self.

"Oh, honey. I have so many insults I could dish at you, but I know you can't take it," Veronica said. She moved in front of Paige and gazed at herself in the mirror. "I look amazing." Paige mentally agreed. Veronica was beautiful. "Jazz will love this dress. I wouldn't be surprised if Rocky sends me a few looks himself."

Paige knew she was trying to get under her skin and she refused to participate. "You look great, Veronica." She turned to walk back toward the dressing room silently begging Meghan to come back over there. Meghan was looking at the dresses on the other side of the store.

"You think he's in love with you? Do you actually think he'll be satisfied with someone like you?"

"Rocky and I are together and frankly it's none of your business."

"You'll never be enough for him. He's destined for greatness and you're just not the kind of girl that can compete with that. You won't be able to hold his attention. You're not enough for him."

Tears burned the back of Paige's eyes. She had been thinking those same things, but hearing it from someone else was like a slap across the face. She hurried back to the dressing room and took the dress off. She just sat there and stared at it for a long time.

Finally, she heard Meghan's voice. "Paige, are you still in there?"

"Yeah," she said.

"What's going on, sweetie? Does the dress not fit? We can get another size if it doesn't."

"No, it's fine," Paige mumbled. She stood and put her clothes back on. She opened the door and handed Meghan the dress.

"What's wrong?" Meghan asked.

"Nothing."

"So, are you buying this dress?"

"No and I'm not going to homecoming. It's just not for me. I'm sure Rocky will understand."

"What happened?" Meghan called as Paige rushed out of the store. She hurried to pay for both dresses and went outside. Paige was sitting in the car just staring off into space.

"Alright, tell me what's wrong and you owe me for this gorgeous dress."

"You shouldn't have bought it. I told you, I'm not going."

"Please, girl. Rocky will bat those beautiful eyes at you and you'll cave." Paige turned a furious look to her best friend. "What happened?" Meghan patiently waited until Paige began to talk.

"Veronica was in the dressing room."

"Oh my gosh. I didn't see her. What did she say?"

"Just stuff that's been bothering me. Like Rocky losing interest or I'm simply not enough for him."

"She only said that because she's so jealous of you. He's crazy about you. Can't you see that?" Paige only nodded her head. She knew he cared about her. "He'll be devastated if you back out on him."

"Really?"

"Of course," Meghan answered.

"Okay, you're right. I don't know why I let her get to me so bad. She irritates me."

"Yes and she knows she does. That's why she does

it," Meghan said. Just then, Paige's phone beeped with a text message.

Can't wait to see you. R

Paige sighed with relief. She shot him a quick text back as Meghan pulled out of the parking lot. She wouldn't worry about the things Veronica said.

Friday nights were always exciting and nerve wracking at the same time. Tonight was their homecoming game. It was halftime and they were down by six points. Rocky was itching to get back out on the field. They were listening to Coach and all his inspiring thoughts and ideas of how they were going to win this game. Rocky knew they could do it.

They each stood up when Coach was finished and was heading back out to the field. Jazz bumped into Rocky.

"What was that for?" Rocky said.

"Do your job, man. Throw a complete pass," Jazz said.

"Do your job and block for me so I can. You're the one letting them all through." Jazz started toward Rocky, but Jake got in the middle.

"Back off, Jazz. Rocky's right. If we lose this game, it will be on you and the line. Not Rocky," Jake said. "The one thing we don't need is for you two to be fighting. We're a team. Act like one."

"Fine," Jazz muttered and walked off.

"Thanks man," Rocky said after Jazz was out of earshot.

"I got your back, but right now, we need you to go

out there and bring you're A game."

"That's what I'm here for," Rocky said. They bumped fists and then took the field. Rocky loved this. The anticipation that hung in the air. All the fans on their feet. This was just high school football, but he loved every minute of it.

He wanted to scan the crowd for Paige, but he had to stay focused. She hadn't let him see the dress or even tell him what it looked like. Of course, it didn't matter to him at all. She could wear an old t-shirt and a jogging pants and she'd still look beautiful to him.

His team huddled up. Rocky called the play. He and Jazz eyed each other for a minute and a silent truce passed between, at least one till the end of this game. They both wanted to win. The ball was hiked. Rocky moved back and spotted Jake. Just before a lineman from the other team got to him. The ball sailed off his fingers and landed beautifully in Jake's arms. He dodged out of the way and watched as Jake made it to the end zone. The crowd erupted in cheers. Yeah, they were changing this game. They were going to win and then he was going to dance the night away with his girl.

Paige sat in Meghan's car. She had been sitting there for several minutes. Finally, Meghan got out and walked over to her side. She pulled the door open.

"Get your cute butt out of my car."

Paige rolled her eyes at her best friend, but she did what she was told. After school that day, Meghan had gone to Paige's house to get ready. They had spent an endless amount of time on Paige's hair and makeup.

Paige wasn't used to that. She'd slipped her dress and heels on and just stared at her reflection in the mirror. She felt exposed in a way she'd never felt before. Meghan's dress was much more revealing than hers, but she still felt like she was on display.

"You look great. Quit worrying," Meghan said as she pulled Paige along. Now, standing in the parking lot, Paige wondered why she even wanted to go to this dance anyway. She breathed a silent prayer, asking God to give her strength. She hated feeling embarrassed.

They walked toward the ball field just in time to see Jake make a touchdown. Everyone was screaming and Paige and Meghan laughed at the excitement. It was hard not to get excited. She watched Rocky. He looked so determined out on the field.

They next thing Paige knew, the game was over and they had won. The band was playing a victory song. Everyone was on their feet. The cheerleaders were going crazy. Some people were even running down on the field.

Paige didn't. Rocky had told her to meet him in the lobby of the school, so she and Meghan walked up to the school and stood talking. Some people stopped to chat with them as they were going into the homecoming dance. Paige started to get nervous again. They heard the football players before they saw them.

Jazz, with his arm around Veronica walked up the hall and into the dance. Veronica sent a heavy glare Paige's way, but she didn't let it bother her. Next, Roman and Molly walked in. Meghan's eyes stayed on them just a little longer. Paige couldn't help but wonder why. The footballs players all filed in and the last two were Jake and Rocky.

Jake walked up to Meghan and smiled. "You ready?"

"Sure," she said and winked at Paige.

Rocky was standing there just staring at her. "What?" she asked.

"You take my breath away," he said. She blushed at that. He had on a pair of khaki dress pants, and a button down dress shirt. He looked great. He walked up to her and slid his hands around her waist for a moment.

"You look good, too," she said. He grinned and grabbed her hand in his. He pulled her along into the dance. It was loud in there. A lot of people were dancing. Everyone was talking at the same time.

"Fun, huh?" he asked.

"Yeah," she said, but sounding very unsure. He laughed at her. "We don't have to stay long."

"Of course we do. We all know who will be homecoming king," Paige said. He rolled his eyes.

"Can we just skip that part?" he asked. Paige laughed at him. He pulled her out on the dance floor and they started having a great time. Paige forgot about being self-conscious. She forgot to worry about anyone else but Rocky. He was all she could see.

Then, Principal Ball picked up the microphone on the stage and cleared his throat. The music stopped and everyone quietened down and turned to look at him. Meghan and Jake had made their way beside Rocky and Paige. Rocky was standing behind Paige with his arms around her.

"As you all know is customary at Valley High, we crown a Homecoming King and Queen and they share a dance. So, our 2015 Valley High Homecoming Queen is…. Veronica Staples." People started clapping and she had the audacity to act surprised. She walked up on stage and blew a kiss to Rocky. Principal Ball placed a tiara on her head.

"Let's get out of here," Rocky said, tugging on Paige's hand.

"Rocky, you know you'll be crowned king. You can't just walk out."

"And our 2015 Homecoming King is Rocky West. Come on up here, Rocky."

"Go," Paige said. Rocky reluctantly let go of her hand and walked up on stage. Principal Ball placed a crown on his head.

"Alright, it's the King and Queens' dance, people."

Rocky stared at Veronica without moving toward her. She grabbed his hand and pulled him toward the dance floor. A song started playing and Veronica put her arms around his neck. They started swaying slowly to the music. Rocky kept his eyes on Paige. He didn't want to see an insecure look cross her face. This was crazy. He didn't want to dance with Veronica.

"Look, I don't mean to be rude, but I just want to dance with my girl," Rocky said.

"Oh my gosh, Rocky. This is tradition. It's not going to kill you to dance with me for one song."

"Fine," he said.

"You know, it used to be me and you."

"I know, but it's not that way anymore."

"Don't you remember how good things were between us?"

"I remember fighting with you and partying with you," he said. "Neither of those things were very appealing."

"Wow, can you be any meaner?" Veronica asked.

"I don't mean to be. I'm just telling you the truth," he said. He chanced a glance at Paige again, but she was talking to Meghan.

"Fine, let me remind you of how good things were," she said. Before Rocky knew what she was doing, she was kissing him. He heard a distinct gasp as he jerked away from her. He turned to Paige and she looked horrified. She ran out of the dance before he could get to her.

"Let her go, Rocky. We belong together," Veronica said, grabbing a hold of his arm.

"Get off of me, Veronica and don't ever talk to me again," Rocky said. He ran out of the dance after Paige but someone from behind knocked him down.

"Get off of me," Rocky said, while trying to turn around to see who'd tackled him.

"You think that's cool man? Kissing my girl?" Jazz slurred.

"Are you drunk?"

"Naw," Jazz said.

"You smell like beer. Come on man, you're at a school function. What's wrong with you? Besides, I didn't kiss your girl. She kissed me and I jerked away from her. I don't have time for this, Jazz. I've got to find Paige."

"Stay away from Veronica, Rocky."

"With pleasure," Rocky said. He turned and scanned the parking lot and spotted her quickly. He ran to her. She was standing by Meghan's car. He knew she heard him, but she didn't turn around.

"Paige?" he said. She didn't answer him. "Baby, I'm so sorry. It wasn't me. She kissed me and I jerked away." She finally turned around and looked at him.

"I know that," she answered.

"You do? Then, why did you run?"

"It just shocked me and I didn't know how to handle it."

"I don't want to kiss anyone but you," he said. He walked closer and took her hands in his. "Do you want to get out of here?"

"Please," Paige said. They walked over to his car, hand in hand. He opened the door for her and then looked back up toward school. He could see Jazz and Veronica arguing. He was glad they were leaving. He wasn't in the mood for all this drama. All he wanted to do was spend some time with his girl.

CHAPTER FOURTEEN

Paige held Rocky's hand as they drove. He continued to apologize and try to explain something that wasn't his fault. Paige stroked her thumb over his knuckles and smiled.

"Rocky, it's fine," Paige said.

"No, it's not. I'm sorry."

"No more apologies. Let's talk about something else, like you how you rocked that game," Paige said. That finally got a smile out of him.

"Yeah?"

"Oh yeah. I was so impressed." Rocky laughed when she said that. He lifted her hand and kissed the back of her soft skin.

"The team played great tonight," he said.

"You played great," Paige said. He picked up her hand and kissed the back of it again. She smiled at him. Just then, a car right behind them flashed their bright lights on. Rocky squinted a little and adjusted his mirror.

"Man, I wish they would dim their lights a little," he

said, but pulled his attention back to the road. "So, you just want to ride around for a while?"

"Sure," she said.

"Okay, maybe if I turn down this next road to the right, that car will go on," he said.

"Yeah, sounds good. They're driving really close to us. Talk about riding your bumper," Paige said. Rocky gave plenty of warning he was turning and then slowed down. The car behind them ran right up on them. Rocky turned on the road to the right. They heard wheels screeching and then the car was behind them again.

"That's weird," Paige commented, glancing in her side mirror.

"Yeah, a little too weird."

"What do you mean?"

"Jazz was outside when we left. It might be him following us. I can outrun him."

"Oh gosh, Rocky, I don't know."

"Okay, I won't. We'll just go to your house. He'll leave us alone then." Just as he was saying that, the car behind them slammed into the back of Rocky's corvette. Paige lunged forward a bit, but her seat belt caught her. Rocky instinctively threw his arm out in front of Paige.

"Rocky," she said with alarm in her voice. She glanced over at him, but he had a fierce look on his face.

"It's going to be okay. Let's get out of here," he said. He mashed the gas and started leaving the other car behind, but it quickly caught up and pulled up to the side. Rocky glanced over and it was Jazz and Veronica. He shook his head with a frustrated look on his face. Then, he slammed on the breaks while Jazz and Veronica kept going.

"He's drunk. I can't believe he's driving and with

another person in the car," Rocky said. He quickly turned the car around and started heading back the way they came. Paige was fidgeting with her hands. She was nervous. It was only a matter of minutes until Jazz had turned and caught back up to them. He pulled up beside of Rocky and started honking the horn. Veronica was laughing. He started swerving toward Rocky's car. He almost ran them off in the ditch, but Rocky was able to keep the car out of it and slid back into the road. Then, up ahead a car's lights shined coming toward them.

"Oh no, Rocky," Paige screamed. She started holding her breath. It was like time stood still for Rocky and everything was going in slow motion. Jazz wasn't looking where he was going at all. They heard a horn blow and Jazz looked up and swerved off the road and then back on. At the last minute, the car coming toward them came over in Rocky's lane and he tried to dodge it. The last thing Paige remembers was flying through the air still holding on to Rocky's hand, hearing a loud crunch and then everything went black.
Paige woke up to a stranger asking her a question over and over again. Ma'am, ma'am, are you okay?" She forced her eyes open and looked up at this stranger standing there. She hurt and for a moment was disoriented. Then, she remembered the crash and sat up quicker than she should have. Her vision was blurry and she had a horrible pain in her head and side. She swayed a little and had to lie back down.

"Rocky?" she said and turned to see her boyfriend unconscious. There was blood everywhere. "Oh my gosh, Rocky. Wake up." Rocky didn't move. Paige could feel tears coming down her face. "Rocky, Rocky, wake up. Please. Please wake up. I need you. Please."

"Ma'am, I'm so sorry. I didn't mean to swerve in your lane. The other car was coming. It was just a reflex."

"Call 911," Paige blurted out, wondering why he hadn't already done that. "Rocky, come on, honey, please wake up." Still, he didn't move. She checked his pulse and it was slow, but there. She breathed a sigh of relief. She hadn't lost him yet. She wasn't going to lose him.

Please God, heavenly father, don't let him die. Lord, we need you right now. Please help us make it through. I'm scared, God. Help me. Please, please help me. Paige prayed and prayed until she heard a loud groan from outside.

"Help. Help me. Someone please help me," Jazz screamed. Paige's insides curled at hearing him scream.

"I'm calling 911," Paige heard the stranger tell Jazz.

"Hang on, baby. I'll be right back. Don't give up. Help's on the way," Paige said. She pushed the door open and got out of the car. She swayed a little on her feet and had to push the nausea down. She held on to the side of the car while she tried to put one foot in front of the other. Paige could feel glass in her head and blood was rolling down the side of her face. It felt warm and sticky.

"Paige, where's Rocky?" Jazz said, running over to her. His arm looked out of joint by the way hung limp at his side. "I need help. I can't pull Veronica out of the car. She hasn't woken up yet."

"He can't help you. He's unconscious, you idiot" Paige screamed at him. She wanted to yell a lot more at him, but she was barely standing up.

"Is he okay?" Jazz said. He looked scared and it

made Paige all the more furious.

"I don't know," Paige said. "He's not moving, but he has a pulse."

"They're on the way," the stranger said. Paige could already hear the sirens in the background. She walked back down to the car and got back in the passenger side. She took hold of his hand.

"I hear the sirens. Help is on the way, baby. Everything's going to be okay," Paige told him. Still Rocky never moved. Paige felt her tears still running down her face. When the ambulance pulled up, they took Veronica first. Paige wanted to scream at them, but then the paramedics came down and started working on Rocky. They eased him out the car and placed him on a stretcher. A paramedic looked her way.

"Honey, are you okay?" he asked. That was the last thing Paige heard as she passed out.

Paige woke up to a strong smell. Someone was waving something in front of her nose. She blinked and tried to focus on the light above her. Where was she? She heard a beeping sound to her right side.

"How are you feeling?" she heard someone asked her. Paige looked around and she saw a nurse standing at her bedside.

"I've been better. Where am I?" Paige asked. She moved to touch her head, but the nurse stopped her.

"Valley Hospital. Do you remember what happened?"

"Um..we were at the homecoming dance and then we left and...oh my gosh...where's Rocky?"

"Who?"

"My boyfriend. He was unconscious. Please, I have to go see him." Paige tried to push herself up, but the nurse pushed her back down on the bed. Paige couldn't put up much of a fight. She was extremely weak.

"Young lady, you need to lay here right now and focus on getting yourself better," the nurse said. "I'll get the doctor."

"No. I need to see Rocky. Please. Is he okay? Where is he? Please. I have to know." Paige's pleas fell on deaf ears. The nurse left the room and came back in a moment with a man who looked to be in his late fifties. He wore glasses on the tip of his nose and stared down at her. His face was blank.

"Hello, Ms. Jones. I'm Dr. Lawson. You've had quite the ordeal tonight. Let me check you out."

"No. Tell me where my boyfriend is right now. Someone tell me," Paige screamed.

"Young lady, if you don't calm yourself down. I will put something in your IV to make you sleep," he threatened. Paige quietened then. She was still furious that no one was telling her where Rocky was. He checked her eyes, listened to her chest and felt her ribs. "You have several cracked ribs and unfortunately, there's nothing we can do for that. They will heal, but there'll be some pain. You have a slight concussion. We retrieved the glass from your head and I stitched up the cuts. I've put a bandage on it for now, but by tomorrow, you can take that off. Just be careful for several days. I want you to follow up with your regular doctor next week." Paige only nodded her head, but that act only made her head throb even more.

"I think there's someone out here demanding to see

you," the nurse said and smiled. Paige perked up then. Maybe it was Rocky. She waited until the nurse came back, but her mom walked in. Ellen burst into tears when she saw Paige.

"Sweetheart, you scared me to death. Don't you ever do anything like this again," Ellen scolded Paige. She wanted to tell her mom it wasn't her fault, but right now wasn't the best time to get into the details with her mom.

"I'll try not to, Mom." Ellen was crying all over Paige's shoulder and although Paige hated to tell her mom, her side was killing her. "Mom, my ribs." Ellen jumped back.

"Oh sweetie, I'm sorry," she said. Her hands fluttered over Paige, like she wanting to make sure she was there and okay, but not wanting to touch her and hurt her again. Finally, she stopped and just stared at her daughter.

"Mom, where's Rocky?" Paige asked.

"Didn't the doctor tell you?" Ellen asked.

"No, he didn't tell me. How is he? Can I see him?"

"He's in ICU right now. He still hasn't woken up."

"He's going to be okay, right?"

"I hope so, sweetie."

The nurse walked in and told them the doctor was discharging her with some pain meds and strict bed rest for the next couple of days. She told Paige she didn't need to be watching TV or reading. She just needed the rest. She told her to lie in a dark room. She took the IV out of Paige's arm and placed a gauze and a piece of tape there. Then, she left for Paige to get dressed.

"I'll be glad to get you home," Ellen said.

"I'm not going home, Mom. I'm going to Rocky."

"You heard the nurse. You need rest."

"I'll get rest after I know Rocky's okay. If it was me, he would be here," she said. "Please, Mom."

"Fine, but at least speak to your friends," Ellen said. "What?"

"I think the entire high school is here in the waiting room," Ellen said. Paige quickly got dressed and followed her mom out to the waiting room. Meghan jumped up when she saw Paige and ran to her. Jake was close behind.

"Paige, are you okay? Where's Rocky? What happened?" Meghan questioned.

"I'm okay. There was a wreck. Rocky's still in ICU. I'm headed there now," she answered.

"Then, we're staying here. If you need us, we'll be here," Meghan said.

"You don't have to do that," Paige said.

"You're my best friend. I'm not leaving here until you do," she insisted.

"Hopefully, I can talk her into going home after she sees him," Ellen said. Paige just smiled up at her mom and then walked back toward the ICU. Holding back her tears was only making her head hurt worse. When she got to his room, she stopped in the door. She saw him hooked up to several machines. She saw his mom, laying her head on the bed beside him while she sat in a rocking chair. His dad was standing. She cleared her throat and both Rocky's parents turned to look at her.

"You must be Paige," Rocky's mom said. She stood and walked over to her.

"May I see him, Mrs. West?" Paige asked.

"Of course, and please, call me Candace," she said. Paige nodded her head and walked to his bedside. She took his hand and the tears started to fall again.

"We'll give you a moment," Rocky's dad said and motioned for Candace to follow him. After they walked out of the room, Paige sat down in the chair beside the bed.

"Hey. It's me. We're okay. We're going to be okay. I'm here. I'm not leaving you," she said. The door opened back up and her mom told them they were going down to the cafeteria for a cup of coffee and they'd be right back. Paige only nodded and then turned her attention back to Rocky. She stroked his hand and arm. "I'd feel much better if you'd just wake up and talk to me."

There was a knock at the door and Paige turned to see Jazz standing in the doorway. She stood. A fury like she'd never felt before raged up in her and she stormed toward the door, pushing him back out into the hallway. She noticed his arm was in a sling, but she didn't care.

"Easy, Paige," Jazz said.

"You just have a broken arm?"

"Yeah. How's Rocky?"

"Unconscious. How does he look?" Paige screamed.

"Look, I just wanted to come here and tell him I was sorry."

"Sorry," she yelled. "Sorry. You can forget it. If I have my way, you'll never talk to him again." She hadn't noticed the door had come open while they were arguing.

"Paige," she heard his voice say. It was weak, but Paige would know Rocky's voice anywhere.

She turned and ran back into the room. He was looking right at her.

"You're awake," she said.

"Yeah. Kind of hard not to be. You were

screaming," he said and tried to chuckle as he teased her.

"I was so worried," Paige said and took his hand in hers.

"Are you okay?" he croaked out.

"Yeah, I'm fine."

"You don't look fine," he said.

"Well, I'll let that one slide," Paige said and smiled at him. He chuckled again, but then winced in pain.

"I think laughter is out of the picture for a while," he groaned.

"Rocky?" Jazz's hesitant voice said behind Paige.

"Go away," she said.

"Hey. It's okay. Let him say what he's got to say," Rocky stated.

"It's not okay," Paige said.

"Come on. Give us a minute," Rocky said. Paige nodded her head, but shot a glare in Jazz's direction.

"I'll be right outside," Paige said and then leaned over and kissed his forehead. She turned and walked out in the hall and shut the door behind her. After she left, they were both silent.

"You came here to talk. Spill," Rocky said.

"I don't know where to begin," he answered. "I've screwed up big time. I've made a mess of my life. Veronica's life. I could have killed my best friend and his girl. I don't know what's wrong with me."

"How is Veronica?" Rocky asked.

"She's not good, man. She's in ICU, too. She's unconscious. Her legs are broken but she has swelling on the brain. She wasn't wearing her seatbelt. Her head went through the windshield. She has a brain injury. They're going to do surgery on her within the hour."

"That doesn't sound good," Rocky commented.

"I've already spoken to the police. They tested my blood when I came in. I was over the legal limit of alcohol in the blood and I'm a minor. If something happens to Veronica, I'm looking at manslaughter or worse."

"She'll be okay," Rocky said. "We have to believe that. As far as the other stuff, you do the crime, you do the time."

"Wow. Thanks for that."

"I'm not sugarcoating anything, Jazz. You chose to drink. You chose to get behind the wheel and even allowed Veronica to ride with you."

"I know. I know. I've been beating myself up ever since we got here. I can't stand the thought she might die. I can't stand the thought that I hurt you. I'm sorry, Rocky. I'm really sorry. I've been jealous of you and I lashed out in the worst possible way. When you started paying attention to Paige, no one else mattered."

"That's not true, man. It's just things changed. I changed. I don't want to drink and party anymore. I accepted the Lord into my heart. I got saved, Jazz."

"I don't know what to say to that," Jazz admitted.

"Think about it. I was the same as you. I was searching for something, but I was looking in all the wrong places. I found exactly what I was looking for in Jesus Christ."

"Yeah well, I'm not really sure what that even means. I just wanted you to know how sorry I am and I hope we can call a truce."

"Yeah, this is over," Rocky said.

"Do you think we'll ever be friends again?" Jazz asked.

"I want to say yes. I hope so, man. Just know I'm

praying for you and Veronica," Rocky responded.

"Thanks," Jazz said and then walked out of the room. Paige rushed back in and sat down beside of Rocky.

"What did he want?" she asked.

"To apologize," Rocky said.

"Do you think he meant it?" Paige asked.

"Yeah, I do," he said and picked up her hand and kissed it. She smiled. "Go home and get some rest."

"No, I'm not leaving you."

"Yes, you are. They will give me something to sleep and then I won't even know you're here. Please, go home. Rest and be back first thing in the morning."

"I don't know what I would have done if I'd lost you," Paige admitted.

"So, you kind of like me, huh?" he asked, teasing her again.

"I love you, Rocky West," she said. Her heart was in her eyes. It should have scared her how quickly she told him that, but it didn't. Tonight had put everything in perspective for her. She loved him and she wasn't letting him go.

"I love you, too, Paige Jones. I'm here. You've not lost me and you're not going to." Just then, his parents along with Paige's mom walked in the room with cups of coffee.

"Rocky? Oh sweetie. You've come back to us," Candace said.

"Hey, mom." Candace broke down in tears seeing her son's eyes open and him talking to her.

"I wasn't here when you woke up," she scolded herself.

"My girl was looking out for me," he said and winked at Paige. Candace reached out and grabbed

Paige's hand.

"Thank you." Paige only nodded.

"I'll see you in the morning," Paige told him. He nodded at her and then Paige and her mom walked out of his room.

Ellen put an arm around her daughter. "Come on, sweetie. Let's get you home and in the bed. I'll bring you back over here first thing in the morning."

As they walked past Veronica's room, they could hear her mom crying. Jazz was standing outside the door with his head bent down.

"What's going on?" Paige whispered to her mom.

"They've taken Veronica in for surgery. It's pretty serious."

"I didn't know," she answered.

"Come on, Paige. It's time for me to take care of you for a while." Paige let her mom lead her out of the hospital and to the car to go home.

CHAPTER FIFTEEN

The next morning, Paige was at the hospital around 7:00. She walked into Rocky's room to see his dad asleep in the chair on the right side of the bed. His mom was on his left side of the bed, half in a chair and half on the bed beside Rocky, who seemed to be sleeping soundly. She had his hand clutched in hers. Paige couldn't help but tear up a little. Candace woke up when she walked closer to the bed.

"Oh, Paige, sweetie, I'm glad you're here. Every time he's woke up, he asked about you," she said.

"I shouldn't have left," Paige said.

"Nonsense. You needed the rest. He's just a little disoriented when he first wakes up," she answered.

"I can sit with him if you need a break," Paige offered.

"Thank you, sweetie. I think I'll take a walk and get us some coffee, if I can get his dad to wake up." Candace and Paige both laughed a little as Mr. West snored from the chair he was sprawled out in. Candace woke him up and they left Paige alone with Rocky. She sat down at his bedside and took his hand in hers.

"Hi, Rocky," she said. She clutched his hand tightly until she felt him squeeze back. Her eyes flew up to his and he was smiling at her.

"Good morning, beautiful," he said. Paige knew beyond a shadow of a doubt she didn't look very beautiful this morning. The gash in her head had stitches and half of her face was blue from the bruises. There were dark circles under her eyes from not being able to sleep because she was worried about him.

"How are you feeling?" Paige asked.

"I'm okay. I'm sore and my head is throbbing, but other than that, I think I'm good. I'm hoping Mom and Dad will spring me today. How's my girl?"

"Better now that I'm here with you," Paige answered. She could feel the tears stinging the back of her eyes again. She could have lost him. It was only by God's grace they had survived and were okay. She knew things could have been a lot worse, but she was really shaken up.

"Hey. None of that. We are okay. Both of us," he said.

"I could have lost you," she said. Her voice cracked a little when she said that and a single tear slid down her face. He reached up and brushed it away.

"Yeah, but you didn't. I'm right here. I'm fine. You're not going to lose me. God was with us, Paige. He knew what was going to happen before it did and he made sure we were okay."

"You're right. I'm just rattled, I guess," she answered. She visibly took a deep breath and smiled at him.

"I love you, Paige Jones," he said and stroked her cheek with his hand. She leaned in closer to him.

"I love you, too," she murmured.

His parents and Ellen walked in then and Paige stood up, but Rocky wouldn't let go of her hand.

They had coffee for everyone and all sat around talking until the doctor came by. He told them they were getting the release papers ready for Rocky to go home, with strict instructions for him to take it easy. He wasn't going back to school for at least another week and football was off the table for the rest of the year. Several of his ribs were broken and he was going to be in a lot of pain for a while. His concussion was better, though. Paige was so thankful for that.

"I guess you need to get dressed, son," Rocky's dad said. Candace, Paige and Ellen stepped outside to give him some privacy. Paige heard a woman crying down the hall.

"Who is that?" Paige asked.

"It's Veronica's mom," Candace answered.

"How is she?"

"In a coma," Candace said. "It's medicine induced to keep her still. The surgery went well, but she has a long recovery ahead of her.

"I think I might head down and see her," Paige said.

"Honey, that's not necessary. You don't owe her anything," Ellen said, looking like a momma bear wanting to protect her cub.

"I know, Mom, but it's the right thing to do," Paige answered.

"Okay. Do you want me to come with you?" Ellen asked.

"No. I won't be long. Tell Rocky I'll be back in a

moment," she said. Ellen and Candace both nodded and watched as Paige walked down the hall and rounded the corner. She walked up to Veronica's room and knocked on the door. An older version of Veronica came to the door and opened it. Her makeup was smeared down her face where she'd been crying. Her hair was messy and she looked as tired as Paige felt.

"Can I help you?" the woman asked.

"Um..I was just wanting to check on Veronica," Paige said.

"I'm sorry. We've not met. Are you one of Veronica's friends?" the lady asked. Paige stared at her for a few minutes, not really sure what to say.

"No, I'm not," Paige answered.

"Then, what are you doing here?" the lady asked.

"My name is Paige," she started.

"Oh, you're that girl," the woman replied. "I really don't think it's a good idea for you to see Veronica."

"I really want to, ma'am. I need to say something to her," Paige responded.

"There's nothing she needs to hear from you. She's in really bad shape and a tongue lashing from you isn't going to help matters any."

"No, that's not it at all. I really want to see her. Please. Can you give me just one moment?"

"Fine. I'm not sure she can even hear you," the woman stated. "By the way, I'm Victoria, her mom." Victoria pushed the door open and let Paige walk in. When Paige looked at Veronica lying helpless in the bed, she didn't feel angry. She only felt pity for the girl. She had a tube down her throat and her entire head was wrapped. Her face was pale and she looked very small. Veronica had always been larger than life to Paige, but now, she was just a girl who needed a lot of prayer. "Go ahead," Victoria said.

"Hey, Veronica. It's Paige. I guess I'm the last person you expected to hear from. I didn't really plan on coming to see you, but I felt like I needed to. You see, God wanted me to come down here and talk to you. I've been angry with you, but I'm not anymore. I just want to tell you one thing. I forgive you." Paige paused when Victoria started to cry again. "I forgive you for everything. For making fun of me, for doing things to me, for trying to make me feel like I wasn't good enough, I forgive you. I want you to get better, Veronica. You have a lot of life ahead of you. I don't know if we'll ever be friends, but I really hope we can stop being enemies. I want you to know, I'm praying for you. I probably won't be back to see you, but you'll be in my prayers every day. Goodbye, Veronica." Paige turned toward Victoria and then walked toward the door.
Victoria followed her out and reached for Paige. She was surprised when Victoria hugged her, but she embraced her.

"Thank you. Thank you so much for that. I know Veronica isn't your favorite person, but thank you for everything you said."

"I meant it. I'll be praying for her and you too."

"You don't know what that means to me."

"Goodbye, Victoria."

"Bye, Paige."

When she walked back around the corner, Rocky was already coming out of the room in a wheelchair.

"I'm fine," he said to one of the nurses. "I can walk to the car."

"Well, the doctor insisted on the wheelchair until you

get outside so you're going to live with it, Quarterback," the nurse responded. He shook his head.

"At least I'm going home," he mumbled. When they went through the front door, Rocky's dad had their car pulled up to the front. "Come over?" he asked Paige.

"Sure," she said and glanced to her mom.

"Call me later and I'll come get you," Ellen said.

"You're welcome to come as well, Ellen," Candace said.

"Thank you, but no. I've got some errands to run," Ellen said and then waved to all of them.

After the ride to Rocky's house and getting him inside, they were finally alone together on the couch. Candace was fixing some lunch and Rocky's dad had some paperwork he needed to get done. Rocky was clicking through the channels trying to find something good to watch on TV. Paige was just content to be curled up next to him.

"Do you think there's a reason for everything?" Rocky asked.

"Yes, I do," Paige answered.

"What good can come out of this wreck?" Rocky asked.

"I'm not sure, but I know God has a purpose for everything," she said. "We may not understand it now, but one day we will."

"How did you get to be so smart?" he asked, teasing her a little. She grinned up at him.

"So, you kind of like me, huh?" she said, repeating the words he'd said to her in the hospital. He turned toward her.

"No, I love you," he said and kissed her. Paige melted into the kiss. When the kiss was over, she rested her head on his shoulder.

"I think we should pray and thank God for being with us," Rocky said.

"Okay, do you want me to pray?" she asked.

"Well, do you care if I do it?" he asked.

"I would love that," Paige answered. She held his hand and closed her eyes as he began to pray.

"Dear Heavenly Father, I just want to thank you for everything. You were there before we wrecked and during the whole ordeal. You watched over us. You kept us from getting injured any worse than we were. You had your hand on us the entire time. I praise you for that. Lord, I want to thank you for saving my soul and giving me a chance to live my life for you. Thank you for bringing Paige into my life. Lord, watch over Veronica and Jazz. Help them heal, but most importantly, show them there's another way to live their lives. In Jesus name, Amen."

Paige stayed snuggled up to his side as they began to watch TV. They had been through a lot, but God had seen them through. He would always be there for them and Paige could take comfort in knowing he was looking after all of them.

EPILOGUE

Rocky and Paige pulled into the school parking lot for the first time after the wreck. Rocky's car had been totaled, so he was driving Paige's. He parked in his regular spot and they were both bombarded with people as they got out of the car. Rocky's friends were coming over, telling them how glad they were to see them and that they were okay. They didn't treat Paige like an outsider anymore.

Once the crowd had thinned, they headed into school, but Rocky stopped just as they walked in the door. He had his arm around Paige, so she stopped as well.

"Everything okay?" she asked.

"Yeah, everything's great. I'm back in school. I have the best girl any guy could ask for, but most importantly, I have God on my side."

"I love you, Rocky West."

"I love you, too, my beautiful Christian girl," he said and dropped a kiss on her nose before they walked to their class together.

Paige knew in her heart God had led Rocky straight into her life and she would thank him every day for that and all his other blessings.

THE END

COMING SOON in 2016
Forgiven Girl

Veronica had always been a mean girl. She loved how she intimidated over half of the student body at Valley High. She wanted people to envy her. She thrived off of chaos, but one fateful night, things changed. A crash. A coma. She had injuries and faced multiple surgeries. Through all of that, there were three words she couldn't forget. I forgive you. She'd heard it, but she didn't know what to do with it. She knew she couldn't go on as the person she once was, but she had no idea who she was supposed to be.

Jake had never liked Veronica. She was his least favorite person in the entire school. After she returned to school, he accidentally overheard a conversation between her and one of her friends and he felt something he never knew he could feel toward her. Pity. She was lost. He offered to listen if she ever needed to talk and she took him up on that. Jake starts to realize she isn't the awful person he thought and finds they have a connection he can't explain.

Can he overcome his bad opinion of her past to truly be there for her?

Will Veronica accept his help and see there's more than just friendship underneath her feelings for him?

Trish Shaver

Made in the USA
Charleston, SC
21 November 2016